Praise for Lilith Saintcrow . . .

"Darkly compelling, fascinatingly unique. Lilith Saintcrow offers a breath-taking, fantastic ride."

—*NYT* bestselling author Gena Showalter

"In the *Watchers* series, Saintcrow writes stories that are almost always nonstop action from beginning to end. Her women are kick-ass strong, her men ruggedly handsome and dedicated to the women they serve. It isn't a bad combination at all."

—*CJReading*

"I read *Dark Watcher* with growing delight. As chapter followed chapter, I never quite knew what was around the corner."

—*Ebook Reviews*

" . . . a one-of-a-kind author."

—Romantic Times *magazine* on *To Hell and Back*

"The story will keep you on the edge of your seat . . ."

—*KD Did It Edits* on *The Demon's Librarian*

Of Dante Valentine . . .

"Dark fantasy has a new heroine . . ."

—SFX magazine

"Saintcrow snares readers with an amazing alternate reality that is gritty, hip and dangerously mesmerizing."

—*Romantic Times* magazine

"She's a brave, charismatic protagonist with a smart mouth and a suicidal streak. What's not to love?"

—*Publishers Weekly*

"This mind-blowing series remains a must-read for all urban fantasy lovers."

—*bittenbybooks.com*

Books by Lilith Saintcrow

The Watchers

Dark Watcher

Storm Watcher

Fire Watcher

Cloud Watcher

Mindhealer

Finder

The Society Series

The Society

Hunter-Healer

Ghost Squad Novels

Damage

Other

The Demon's Librarian

Damage

A Ghost Squad Novel

by

Lilith Saintcrow

ImaJinn Books

This is a work of fiction. Names, characters, places and incidents are either the products of the author's imagination or are used fictitiously. Any resemblance to actual persons (living or dead), events or locations is entirely coincidental.

ImaJinn Books
PO BOX 300921
Memphis, TN 38130
Print ISBN: 978-1-61194-995-7

ImaJinn Books is an Imprint of BelleBooks, Inc.

Published in the United States of America.

ImaJinn Books was founded by Linda Kichline.

We at ImaJinn Books enjoy hearing from readers. Visit our websites
ImaJinnBooks.com
BelleBooks.com
BellBridgeBooks.com

10 9 8 7 6 5 4 3 2 1

Cover design: Debra Dixon
Interior design: Hank Smith
Photo/Art credits:
Woman (manipulated) © Ammentorp | Dreamstime.com
Background (manipulated) © Crackerclips | Dreamstime.com

:Ldrf:01:

Dedication

To Brenda Chin, with thanks.

. . . pars magna bonitatis est velle fieri bonum.
—Seneca the Younger

At Home

He Believed It

IT WAS A BEAUTIFUL day in the American desert, clear and sunny without a cloud to be seen, but in the bowels of the Shadebrook VA Hospital you wouldn't know it. Fluorescent glow bounced off faintly waxy fields of industrial linoleum, carpeted areas a thin, close-cropped skin of blue and orange nylon, and a tinge of disinfectant shouting *hospital* drained every fraction of good feeling out of a twenty-four-hour interval that already had too little to begin with. This wasn't even a real office, just a cubicle built along the side of a hallway. The temporary partitions, carpeted like the floor but in neutral colors, were three-quarters high and flimsy as paper.

No real cover at all. You'd do better hiding behind a printer—not that you could find one anywhere the patients might get to it.

They were more expensive than warm bodies, after all.

"Physically, you're fine." The buzzcut doctor set the stack of paper aside, his wire-rim glasses glittering. His nametag said *Karsten,* and he had the pink-rimmed blue eyes some blonds were cursed with. It was enough to make your own peepers water, looking at his rabbit-blinking, and he wasn't graying but going white in small patches. His scalp was an angry pink where the buzzers had got near the skin, too. "You're in great shape, First Lieutenant."

Perched on the edge of a hard red plastic chair, Vincent Desmarais leaned forward even further, bracing his elbows on his knees, since he didn't have to even *sit* at attention here. Chestnut hair, just a fraction too long, itched all over his head. He hadn't bothered shaving, so the beard was coming in, gold-tipped. His fingers were numb, maybe because his hands itched to wrap around a throat.

Any throat would do; maybe even this white-coated motherfucker's. Which was a sure sign he was near the edge, if not all the way over and accelerating downward.

Vincent made a neutral noise that could be taken for assent, but the doc seemed to expect more of a response. It was easiest to just parrot the last thing Karsten said, so that's what Vince did.

"Physically. Yeah." He couldn't really argue. He was in fine fucking shape, on the outside; what was there to do when you couldn't sleep except exercise?

"The nightmares, the nosebleeds, the hearing difficulties . . ." Bespectacled Karsten shifted uneasily in his own cushioned chair. The computer screen at his elbow went dark, a headache-inducing screensaver blooming against sudden black blankness. Green lines looping round and round, enough to make a man dizzy if it didn't give him a migraine first. "Combat fatigue isn't anything to mess with."

"Yessir." So now Vince was a cracked plate—couldn't put it through any heat or it'd fracture worse. What was the use of surviving the training *and* the fucking missions, if he wasn't going into the field again? No suit up, strap on, and kiss your ass goodbye. No metallic adrenaline, no grit, nothing that could make a man feel alive instead of like a slowly strangling, sinking corpse.

Nothing, in short, that he wanted.

"I understand you're not very pleased," Karsten continued, pitiless. Vince had to hand it to the man—he had a gift for understatement, that was for damn sure.

Apparently even first lieutenants with heavily redacted files didn't rate a frigid examining room with paper over the table, or even the comfort of hearing this bullshit in an actual office. Just a rabbit-blinking medic in a cubbyhole with three-quarter walls off a heavily traveled linoleum hall, the entire shitheap built under budget constraints for the express purpose of giving men bad news.

Vince's throat was too dry. What came out was a croak masquerading as a normal voice. "How long?"

Karsten acted like he didn't know what his patient was asking, his eyebrows turning into peaked roofs. His teeth were very white and almost perfect despite the faint odor of cigarette smoke clinging to his clothes; he probably sucked on those chemical-taste bleaching strips by the handful. "How long . . .?"

"How long before we—before *I* can go back out?" Vince's teeth kept wanting to grind. It reeked of floor wax and disappointment, pain and disinfectant. *Veterans*, they said. *Broken-down horses* was more like it, used up and put out to pasture.

The last mission hadn't even been that much of a bastard, just a straight retrieval. It had gone smoothly as possible except for Klemp's now-fixed leg, which made whatever was wrong with Vincent even *more* of a mystery. They'd gotten off lightly, everyone in the squad knew it, and the bullet hadn't taken out any of Klemperer's moving parts, just a chunk of thigh.

Hell, the powers that be should've been downright *thankful* Vince was feeling sleepless and savage; it might even add something to his efficiency on the next mission.

Assuming they ever gave him another one. And thinking of his squad going out with someone else in command—someone who didn't understand Klemp wouldn't want to be left stateside or Boom's sardonic humor, Tax's compulsive gear-checking, Grey's need for clear guardrails, *or* Jackson's quiet—was unpleasant at best.

He *had* to clear this. There was no other option.

"It depends." At least Karsten didn't try to sugarcoat it further. "Six months is the standard for re-evaluation in cases like this to make sure it's just battle stress and not PTSD." He spread his hands. Nice, soft palms, a too-tight gold wedding band, buffed nails—oh, you could tell the good doctor kept himself far, far away from the mud and the blood. He probably played tennis for exercise; racquetball or squash instead of pounding leather on rest marches. "Sometimes all it takes is time. There's therapy, and I'd like to get you on an antidepressant to even out the mood swi—"

Vincent stiffened. A shrink and pills? No fucking *way*. "Six months. You've got to be kidding." He'd lose his edge, sitting for that long. Here he was, in jeans and a T-shirt like a goddamn civvie. What he really wanted was fatigues, webbing, and the simplicity of a job to be done.

At least he had his boots, laced high and just tight enough. There was no foreign sand left in their tread now, but they were familiar. Friendly, even.

Probably the only thing about him that was, at this point.

"That's the regular timeframe." Karsten sighed, probably used to delivering unwelcome news to big-shouldered jarheads. Maybe they even gave him a bonus for the troublesome ones. "You could even study up for your next promotion. Look, I understand you don't like it—"

You don't understand shit, doc. "Fine. Six months." Vince stood up too fast, unfolding fluidly, and the doctor leaned back a little. It would be easy to make a fist. He wouldn't even have to hit the jackass, just send his knuckles through the computer screen. Or even through the divider masquerading as a wall. What would they do then, stockade or antidepressants? It was anyone's guess. "Thanks, Doc." *For nothing.*

At least he didn't have to salute before walking away.

"Desmarais. First Lieutenant Desmarais!" Karsten switched to auditory artillery, like a father trying to corral a wayward teen. "*Vincent!*"

Vince left the man standing in the cubicle, and it was a good thing the medic didn't try to follow him. It would be the stockade for sure if the soft dumb bunny laid a hand on him, even *tried* to slow him down. He plunged through the warren of brightly lit halls, retracing his route like a soldier in a minefield, and burst from the air-conditioning into the heavy dry blaze of a southwestern summer without the pop of distant fire or the persistent smell of dung.

It was, after all, the good ol' US of A instead of some other country only Tax or Jackson knew the local language of. Yucca plants raised their spiny heads, and the hills in the distance were shimmering smudges hidden behind overheated air. He scanned the parking lot—cover, sure, but not a lot of it, a light day at the VA. Las Cruces was a smoke-smudge on the horizon, and the heat was a living blanket pressed against sweating, shrinking skin.

Six months. Half a year. He was going to go crazy, especially if they sent the others on a mission without him. He'd parked near a brick retaining wall; his hands were fists, bitten-short fingernails digging in hard. The temptation to go a few rounds with the fucking wall just to prove he could take it was what Grey would call *a bad fuckin' idea, Loot.*

It was, Vince decided as he stepped off the curb and his nape prickled, time to shake Klemp for a job.

PAUL KLEMPERER'S wide, airy almost-adobe apartment building was quiet in the afternoons, civilians at offices, retail work, or maybe even out enjoying the sunshine. Even the retired woman they called the concierge instead of the super—as if they were in fucking France instead of farther west than Texas, ten-gallon hats notwithstanding—was nodding on a bench by the front entrance, sunning her thickened ankles and steel-grey bun. *Just don't ever piss her off,* Klemp had said more than once. *Bitch has a temper.*

It wasn't like Klemp to be afraid of a biddy half his size, but Vincent still kept his nice manners on while visiting. You never could tell, and any old woman who liked sitting outside when it was over ninety degrees deserved to be saluted and then left alone.

Vince took the stairs two at a time, his skin itching and his eyes hot as a barrel after firing; floors passed in a blur. He wasn't winded when he reached the third, but the walls shrank in and it was like he was wearing a helmet again, a fuzzy green night vision glare and his pulse spiking.

Except there was nothing to shoot, and nothing to break. Just the wire getting tighter and tighter, strands popping and fraying all through his bones, nerves worked thinner and thinner, a man turned into hamburger.

There was the red door with its familiar brass 3E; he knocked twice, paused, knocked twice again. That was the signal for *friendly*, or at least, *not a goddamn salesman.*

After a few moments, the locks rattled and a curly-headed, puckish fellow soldier peered through, his hazel gaze gleaming with amusement. The slight, cheerful glimmer was matched by a thick gold chain at a weightlifter's neck; the man was built like a fireplug. "Yo, Dez! My man." Klemp sounded too goddamn happy.

As usual. He was letting his hair grow too, but that meant nothing—he did it on R&R despite the ribbing when he came back wearing a mop.

"Hey." Vincent shouldered past him into a short hall holding the ghost of a steak dinner, a faint fragrance of air freshener, and floor wax, again. Except in here, it was restful. Hardwood, spare dark furniture, white sheers over the windows—it looked like a fucking magazine. "You alone?"

Klemp was a neat little soul, shipshape, everything in its place. If he hadn't been that way naturally, the service would have done it. "Well, I tossed out my supermodel girlfriend this morning, so of course." He stuffed his phone into his ass pocket; Vince looked for where he'd stashed his door-answering weapon and couldn't find it.

"Shoulda let her stay." It was a pale attempt at a joke, one Vince's buddy and putative second-in-command didn't dignify with a response.

Not particularly short but muscle-packed enough to look like it sometimes, Klemp had a slight limp in his banty rooster-walk. The leg was doing fine, but he wasn't going to be sent out for a while either. Not like Paul minded, or if he did, he didn't show it.

"I'll mention it next time I see her." Of course, Klemp being Klemp, he always had more than one iron in the fire. He was a born-fucking-organizer, that was for sure. "What's up?"

What do you think? Vincent stalked into the orange-countered kitchen. The antique fridge wheezed a greeting as he yanked it open, subtracting a beer from a well-supplied shelf. "You still got jobs?"

"Here and there." Paul leaned in the doorway, arms crossed and his brawny forearms fuzzed with dark hair. Soccer jersey, clod boots, and jeans, the uniform of the off-duty and wanting to stay that way. *He* didn't look like he was having trouble adjusting, but then again, this was the same fuckwad who kept smiling and cracking jokes all during dustoff while his leg pumped out claret Tax was having trouble stopping, all the while turning whiter than a sheet. "Sure, help yourself, Loot. What you need?"

"Work." *Something. Anything.* Vincent didn't slam the fridge door, but it was close. The scrapes along his knuckles throbbed—you had to be careful with bricks. A half-wall in a parking lot didn't give a fuck if some flesh-sack hit it. If Vincent fractured his own goddamn fingers it would be his own goddamn fault and it would go in his file, another six months of sitting with his thumb up his ass once they'd figured out he'd lost his temper.

Thankfully, Klemp didn't ask the obvious. He just nodded, his mouth turning into an upside-down U as he mulled it over. When he was thoughtful, he looked like the youngster he'd once been arriving in basic; they hadn't been able to beat the amusement out of him. Even finishing school hadn't, though it had stripped him of thirty pounds in the first few weeks and almost killed Tax.

No, Klemp's sunny optimism was bred in, and couldn't be scrubbed out even with qualification training. He only got serious when the mortars started popping. "Babysitting all right for you?"

"Whatever pays." *And breaks a few bones.* The latter would be more of a bonus, really. Not *absolutely* necessary, but nice.

Even therapeutic. The good old doc would approve of Vincent keeping busy, right?

"All right." Klemp peeled himself upright, dug in the fridge as well. Glass clinked. Outside the window a dog barked, the counterpoint to a lazy afternoon. "Starting when?"

"I've got time." Vince found the church key in its usual drawer, cracked the beer, and tossed the opener to Klemp. Took a long pull. Antidepressants, for God's sake. *Therapy.* Like anything other than a mission would fix the wiring in his head, or the frayed rope in his gut, or the sparking along all his exposed nerves.

"More than a week?" At least Klemp didn't say *no* right away. That meant there was a chance.

"Sure." He didn't even *like* beer, but it was better than nothing. Carbonation filled his nose, and scabs on his stinging knuckles cracked as his free hand curled into a fist.

"Okay." Klemp pretended not to notice, opening his own beer. He also didn't try to say *it wasn't your fault, Loot*, which would have driven

Vince out the door and into the sunshine again. "Shit, man, day drinkin'. Look at you."

"Yeah." Vincent pushed his hip against a counter, glanced at the stove. Nice, bright, scrubbed, and orange as a shag rug. If the living room was a magazine, the kitchen was a seventies time capsule. "Fuck you too, Klemp."

"Not my type, asshole." Klemp laughed like the joke was a good one. Nobody had even ribbed him about not dodging the bullet; it had been entirely too close. "I got a plum of a job, good pay, babysitting for a businessman. Real luxury work, but I don't want to live onsite. You want it?"

"Cash?" Meaning, *what side of the line are we talking?*

Klemp's smile turned upside-down again, but only briefly. "Yeah, but not like it matters." In other words, *no, you're not gonna have to cover something up.* He even took a pull off his own bottle, and belched afterward like the filthy grunt he'd been when they were all young and all the classified work was just a bad dream in some colonel's brain.

"Good enough," Vincent said, and at that point, he believed it.

Break My Heart

"SHH, IT'S ALL RIGHT," Cara Halperin crooned, soothing. Her neck ached; her eyes were hot and grainy. Come to think of it, her back hurt, too—but any woman over thirty knew *that* was inevitable. Eddie insisted on having his bedroom window open a crack despite the air-conditioning; a sweet warm breeze tiptoed through, hay-scented with high summer landscaping and mineral water from the sprinklers.

Sobs shook Eddie's little body. His left fist tangled in her dark hair, pulling tight, and his arms and legs were desperate, clutching vines. His pajamas, blue cotton patterned with trains, were all twisted. He buried his face in her neck and moaned, hot breath a damp spot along her collarbone.

"It's all right," she repeated, conscious of the lie. Nothing was ever all right; why did they tell little kids that? Because it was better than the alternative, or because most adults were dumb enough to want to believe it, perhaps. When you were comforting someone else, it lessened your own terror by a fraction or two.

She swayed, weight shifting from hip to hip. Women at grocery stores did this instinctively, lined up at checkout with tired children in their arms. Other women were in the middle of darkened rooms all over the world, saying the same things, moving exactly the same way.

Except they were cradling their own children, and she was just the nanny. Still, any voice in the night was better than nothing when you were six years old and terrified.

It took about a half hour for Eduardo Marquez to calm down. She paced his room, back and forth—the carpet with streets woven into its pattern, white lines painted with something nontoxic, its nap delightfully short so it wouldn't stall tiny toy car wheels, the big window with its pale-painted iron bars to keep a rich man's possessions safe, the unfinished pine dresser, the race car bedstead with its cheerful red paint and big yellow *#1* painted on the side. She moved into the playroom every few rounds, where everything was neatly put away, but a Lego or two inevitably lay in wait for an unwary bare foot. Her throat burned, matching her eyes, but Eddie calmed down quicker if she spoke. Singing would be better, singing in Spanish best, but his father wanted the poor kid to "improve his English."

It was almost Roman, she mused. A conquering language, especially good for social advancement; Marquez wanted his son firmly in the top crust from childhood. What father didn't want the best for his kid?

Of course, "best" was a relative term. Even for the well-to-do.

Finally Eddie was limp and quiescent, falling back into the deep river of sleep. Cara laid him down, pulled the covers up, and straightened with a sigh, pressing her knuckles into her lower back. Schlepping around a six-year-old was a good workout. Her own pajamas—boxers and a red *Later Days* tank top—bunched in embarrassing places. You couldn't stop to straighten anything when a kid you were responsible for was screaming his lungs out.

Eddie had grown out of most of his baby fat, turning wiry except for a little bit of belly pudge and round cheeks. He lay on his back, mouth slightly ajar, pearly teeth peeping out and his dark curls tousled. His hands were still baby-like, too, their backs smooth, the knuckles mere dimples and his stubby fingers not catching up with the rest of him yet. She smoothed the sheet and the light cotton blanket, knowing he'd get hot and kick all the confining cloth off again.

Three a.m. She closed his bedroom door softly and paused, weighing the trek across the playroom to her own tiny closet. It had a window, sure, a good Ikea bed and a serviceable dresser. But in this expensive, sprawling pile, it was a confining cell. She had a postage stamp-sized bathroom of her very own, and at least it didn't have a camera hidden in the ceiling.

At least, she was reasonably sure it didn't. The thought of the security staff—especially Alan—watching her pee alternated between irritating and bleakly amusing.

Finally, Cara slipped into the hall and took the back stairs to the kitchen. It was as dead and dark as the rest of the house, only the warning red eye on the keypad near the back door blear-blinking its hangover warning. It might have been nice to slip outside and go for a walk, but keying in her code and dealing with Alan asking intrusive midmorning questions was too much of a hassle. Better to wait for five-thirty, like usual, and take her yoga mat out near the pool.

Routine had its own benefits, even if it gave her too much time to think.

Her hair, its ends brushing her mid-back, was a heavy weight. The weather cooled fractionally at night as summer waned, but she was grateful for the refrigerator-intense AC, even if Eddie pleaded for open windows at bedtime. She prowled around the kitchen island, wishing Emilia was in. Even if the cook had stayed overnight, she'd be asleep now, like any decent reasonable person.

Three a.m. belongs to the unreasonable. Cara settled for pouring a glass of milk. It went down easy, and she was halfway through before she realized she hadn't heated it up the way science said would provide a tranquilizing effect.

Par for the course. She sighed, and while she was washing the glass she realized she hadn't thought about . . . *it* . . . in hours. Maybe she was getting better.

The thing was, she didn't want to. She wanted to remember every moment, from the spreading red rosette on the sheets to the sick cramping in her lower belly. The look on the doctor's face, bad news waiting to be delivered, and the sick, squirming terror under Cara's breastbone that refused to go away.

It's what you deserve. What kind of mother forgets that? Ever?

She shook her head, a short sharp motion, and pushed her hair back, replacing the glass in the cabinet with a small click precisely where it had been before. Nothing out of place, everything as it should be.

Then she shuffled back to bed, to stare at the white-painted ceiling until another day's work rolled around.

THE PARK WAS ridiculous. Estates around here were so big you had to drive to get to overwatered grass, a baseball diamond, and top of the line play structures—which kind of defeated the whole purpose of healthy activity, as far as Cara was concerned. Still, you couldn't have the tender spawn of the rich and locally powerful dropping of heatstroke or snatched by largely mythical kidnappers while riding their small, expensive bicycles.

As soon as the black SUV's door closed Eddie was off like a shot, hightailing across bark dust to climb for the burning slide. Later he'd want her to swing with him, but first, she had to let him run off some of that restless energy. Thick, golden sunshine battered through fragile leaves of newly planted saplings, the older trees at the edges of the park too ragged for upscale tastes. Probably like the strips along highways—modesty screens, so you didn't see the clear-cut, baking slopes behind them.

"You were up late." Alan de la Cruz, head of security and her boss's putative right-hand man, pushed his dark, well-worn hat back with a blunt fingertip, squinting at her. His whole Dracula Cowboy thing could have been kind of cute, if you ignored the meanness hiding in his dark eyes and the sloppiness of his stubble. The silver caps on his boot-toes were a strike against him, too.

So you were *on the cameras*. Cara's teeth wanted to grind; she forced her cheeks to relax and shaded her sunglasses with one hand. "That's called voyeurism, Mr. de la Cruz." She set off for her usual bench, and Alan trailed in her wake. It must have been hot in black jeans, black T-shirt, and that jacket of his, but he didn't seem to mind.

Fashion meant suffering even for men, apparently.

There weren't many parents here. Instead, the nannies congregated in what shade they could find, watching their charges and gossiping. There were new faces—Lola and Gertrud were gone, probably back to their home countries. The more expensive agencies weren't supposed to have high turnover, but even someone raised to believe the US was the land of milk and honey could get tired of low pay and bruising hours looking after someone else's spoiled brat. Or brats, plural. That was slightly unfair, since most of the children were sweet enough despite their parents, and the majority of families were reasonable too, even if they treated an *au pair* more like slave labor and a nanny more like a maid.

Nora and Jeanie weren't around—Tuesdays meant ballet for Nora's little Emma, and baby taekwondo for Jeanie's hell-raising twins. So Cara settled alone on her usual bench in thin sapling-shade, watching Eddie zoom around the play structure. He was good about keeping in sight, not like some of the escape artists her fellow nannies complained about. His dark curls bobbed as he streaked from one end of the bark dust to the other, and her chest hurt a little.

She busied herself digging in the large leather bag. Bottled water, wipes, snacks, a comb, spare napkins, a couple books and a slim tablet for games when Eddie had to be kept occupied—the list went on, all the various accoutrements of well-prepared childcare. God forbid a kid *or* employee should ever have time to think or daydream. She pulled out her phone, too.

No messages, but she checked it anyway, just as usual.

And as usual, Alan didn't take the hint. "I was on duty." He settled on the other half of the bench, stretching out his legs and probably glad Nora and Jeanie weren't around to put a crimp in his Casanova routine. It was Nora who'd come up with *Dracula Cowboy*, sending Cara into a fit of giggles unmatched since high school. "Anyway, I didn't tell the señor about it."

You could just call him Mister. You're about as Hispanic as I am, despite that name of yours. Still, it explained why Eddie's dad hadn't shown up at breakfast to grill her about his son's night terrors. She should have suspected it was a mercy she'd pay for later. Cara made a noncommittal noise and kept digging in the bag, rearranging and organizing.

Alan's boot-toes twinkled merrily in the sunshine. He lasted a whole two minutes without poking at her, damn near a record. "You gonna thank me?"

"Why should I? You'll just tell him later." *Especially if you get tired of me saying no.* It wasn't the first time she'd contemplated emailing the agency to ask for a transfer. As usual, the thing that stopped her was Eddie slowing his wild zigzags and turning to glance over his shoulder. His expensive sneakers dug in, throwing up bark chips; he was checking to make sure she was still there, still watching.

Another sharp pain speared her bruised heart. Cara waved and smiled, reassuring him. Right on time, the recognition of her own idiocy arrived as well.

A nanny wasn't supposed to get attached. It was in all the training, how to keep the stupid chunk of cardiac meat in your chest from wrapping its jellyfish tentacles around kids you would never see again. She'd told herself it was desensitization, that it was perfectly normal, but adulthood was knowing better.

"Man, you're hard to please." Alan grinned, wolfish in his hat brim's shade. He was one of those guys who liked chasing the unavailable, and balancing on that edge was second nature for any woman.

There were very few men at the park, and despite the heat, all of them wore jackets like his. Cara tried not to think about it, or about the holster under Alan's left armpit. The guys exchanged glances and small nods whenever they got close to each other, but they didn't talk like the nannies did. One or two even had weird little earbuds she'd never seen outside of movies.

The agency had handouts about what to do if the security measures didn't work, and there was kidnap insurance. Not that parents would mind if the nanny got snatched, but if you were taken with the kid, they might as well try to get both back.

Otherwise the neighbors might talk.

"You have no idea," Cara muttered, and set the timer on her phone for fifteen minutes. Letting Eddie get heatstroke wasn't part of the deal.

"That's okay." Alan's gaze roved the park. All the guys were like that, constantly scanning, as if they expected monsters to pop out of sparse underbrush. It made her tired just watching that constant alertness. "Señor likes you. None of the others stayed this long."

Did you harass them too? "Mh." Another noncommittal noise. She had several varieties, mostly deployed on Eddie. If she'd known they were this effective on adult males, she would have started using them the moment she hit thirteen. Sarcasm got attention; mild blandness was easier.

"Kid likes you too." Alan was chatty today, relaxed and expansive. His belt buckle was shiny too, and the belt was snakeskin. Or so he said. "He got rid of one by putting garter snakes in her bed."

"Charming," she murmured. If it got bad, there was a Stephen King paperback in the bag. She could pretend to read and maybe he'd leave her alone. "I didn't get much sleep and I'm not in a good mood today, Alan."

"I don't mind at all." Alan offered a saturnine grin, and she got the idea he wanted to move closer on the bench. *That* was why the bag was firmly between them, and partly why it was overstuffed too. "Better ask me on a date soon, though. Dinner in town before the big man goes on his trip?"

Wait, what? "That's news." Her skin felt tight and shiny no matter how much sunscreen she slathered on, and she wondered if taking a posting to Iceland was an option. She could always put on another layer of clothing, but you could only strip so far when it got hot. "Mr. Marquez has a trip coming up?" She tried not to sound overly interested; any crumb would turn the man into a nuisance.

Well, more of a nuisance than he already was.

"After the party, chica." Alan was visibly delighted at breaking the news. He shifted slightly as if the holster under his left armpit needed adjusting. "You're gonna hafta do without me for a few days."

"First good news I've had in months," she muttered. "Thanks for telling me."

"Aw, you're gonna break my heart." Dracula Cowboy's smile vanished. Cara looked hurriedly away, checking on Eddie again. Thankfully, Alan turned sullen after that exchange, and the rest of the time at the park was either full of blessed silence or Eddie's chatter. She even hit the swings with the little guy for a little longer than she'd intended. Maybe that was why she felt dizzy all the way home and later that afternoon, no matter how much water she drank.

At least that night she was exhausted enough to sleep.

Babysitting

BROKEN GLASS AND iron spikes topped the wall around the property; the blunt snouts of cameras sniffed back and forth like surveillance metronomes, and the rest of the setup screamed *money.* A semi-professional, dirty-blond chunk of civilian muscle with a black jacket and a shoulder holster took Vincent's measure at the gatehouse, checked his ID against a clipboard, and waved him through.

The house itself was a mission-style pile with creamy walls and dusty reddish roof-tiles in the grand tradition of more cash than sense. No central courtyard in the sprawl, but the lawns were green with flagrant disregard of drought or water rationing. A pool glimmered cobalt and innocent, cedar Adirondack chairs resting under patterned umbrellas. It practically screamed *first-generation moolah, thanks, and looking to make it past two.* Vincent's black Range Rover was too old and dusty to fit in, so he took a kind of perverse pleasure in pulling around the circular fountain in the middle of the driveway.

His contact was a lean dark-haired guy with shiny-toed cowboy boots and the flat dark eyes of an actual professional who might almost, *almost* make military grade, standing on the expansive white concrete stairs like he owned the place and giving the new arrival a blatant once-over. The motherfucker even had a black cowboy hat, a shiny belt buckle, and a hip-length leather jacket despite the heat. A creature of air-conditioning, or just one of the blessed who didn't sweat much. He didn't look like a show pony, though—there was good muscle in his wiry frame, and he kept his weight balanced evenly.

Interesting. Plus, the jacket was tailored to hide the shoulder holster, a dead giveaway for *ambition.* "Desmarais?" No accent, just a breath of Midwest in the vowels. You could take the boy out of the corn, but not the other way around; his type generally wilted this far west-and-south. "Nice to meet you. I'm Alan de la Cruz."

"Pleasure." Vince didn't try to crush the other man's hand. There was no point, and anyway, Alan didn't try that crap on *him*, either. "Hope I'm not late."

"No worries. Traffic's bad in town." A long, purely European nose and thin lips added to slightly bandy legs; the man could be a greenhorn in a comedy film, ready to go riding the sagebrush and learning important life lessons. Nevertheless, de la Cruz grinned easily at him, a good-natured expression. "You come highly recommended."

Which could have been a lie, or could mean Klemp had warned this cowboy Vincent wasn't a dumbass jarhead on his first off-the-books stint, perfectly legal as long as it didn't interfere with actual military duties. Either way, it worked. "Thanks."

"The other entrance is around the side, but come on in this way." The black hat bobbed as Alan headed up the stairs, one half of the massive front door opening on silent hinges when he applied light, proprietary pressure to the latch. "It's a light assignment. There's a party coming up, and after that, the señor is away for a few weeks on a business trip. Babysitting two packages, the kid and the nanny."

Getting right down to it. Well, Vince didn't like to waste time either. "Nanny?" Klemp hadn't said anything about *that.* And the "other entrance" was undoubtedly for employees.

He was nastily glad he'd parked by the front, at least this time.

"Yeah." Alan didn't remove his hat inside the cool dark foyer, either. Strike one, but it wasn't like Vince cared. Busting a civilian's chops was a fool's game. "Take 'em shopping, to the playground. Keep an eye on them."

Goddammit. Klemp had said *businessman*, not *women and kids.* Maybe it was Paul's idea of a joke, in which case he'd tag the motherfucker next time he saw him. "Sounds like a vacation." Vince scanned the foyer once. The sudden air-conditioning was a frigid relief, and there were pots of decorative silk plant matter. Nothing living, but then again, what would survive in this heavy shade?

"Yeah, well, there's never been a problem." Alan chose a hall and set off; the easy grin didn't match his tense, stiff strides. Either he was ready for anything, or he didn't like a newcomer in what he plainly considered *his* space. "We generally bring in extra help when el señor throws parties."

Parties. Which meant working a room or two. Boring, but still better than sitting at home. "Okay."

"This way. I'll introduce you to the big man."

It was all cool air and dimness, hardwood floors and a few good pieces of pre-Columbian art under recessed spotlights. Either the guy had bought the place furnished or he had a wife with some taste; it looked like a goddamn *Architectural Digest* spread in here. A security nightmare despite the unobtrusive cameras—all sorts of blind spots and corners, the furniture arranged for aesthetics instead of to channel attackers. Wine-red leather, spotless glass, decorative iron grilles over some windows, framed prints matching the furniture instead the other way 'round; it all added up to a man who had laid hands on some initial money and just maybe had the intellectual horsepower to turn it into something more durable.

Vincent was distinctly underdressed. A suit would have done better here, but at least his own jacket was high-quality and subtly different than Alan's. And this de la Cruz had passed enough of Klemp's sniff test to get out of a professional's way.

The king of this semi-castle was a broad man in his fifties and a very good gray suit, his wingtips mirror-polished, his tie subtly patterned, and his thick gold pinkie ring just on the edge of vulgar. The señor—it was impossible to guess what he made his money from, and Vince wasn't enough of a racist to assume the obvious—sat behind a beached whale of a cherrywood desk, a broad, unbarred bay window behind him full of sunshine and a wide expanse of golf-green lawn. "This is the new security?" A pleasant, firm tenor, and Vincent stood to attention.

It never hurt, and most men too cowardly to go into the service liked to think you were *honoring* them when you did it.

"Yessir." Alan's grin looked habitual. "Vincent Desmarais, Mr. Roderigo Marquez."

"Well, welcome." A slow nod, well-manicured fingertips pressing each other as the king measured Vince's duty-boots to his canvas jacket, all the way up to his fresh-shaved cheeks. The minute, unhurried appraisal stopped at all the right spots, which meant Marquez was more than he appeared. "Alan tells me you're a military man."

"Yessir." Vince's throat was dry. If the ubiquitous *thank you for your service* came up he'd have to nod, but thankfully the man chose a less banal option.

"I have a lot of respect for that." Marquez had a nice, fruity voice, used to smooth deals; he stood and offered his hand over the desk. Like his cowboy butler, he had a good firm grip, even if it was too soft for real work. "We'll be paying you in cash, of course."

"Yessir." Vincent fought the urge to duck his head like a kid in front of the teacher. Who brought out cash on the first date, for God's sake? He might just kick Klemp's ass for this one.

Too late to back out now, though. And he wasn't at home watching something forgettable on television or doing pushups, so he'd gotten exactly what he asked for.

"Well, then." Señor's bright, interested gaze clouded as he settled behind his paper-strewn desk again. A sleek black computer hummed, its screen at a precise angle to deny anyone but Marquez a view of its secrets, and a similarly expensive cell phone sat in a small leather-covered tray next to a black landline that looked complex enough to make a cappuccino. Expensive fountain pens in a case, an actual inkwell, and a desk blotter completed the picture of a man serious about his business, whatever that was. "Alan will show you around, get you settled."

"Thank you, sir." It cost nothing to be polite, and maybe he'd even get a good story out of this. Grey would want to hear about the house, Tax about the cameras, and Jackson would get a good laugh out of Alan's shiny boot-toes.

But the señor nodded, turning back to his computer, and just like that, Vince and the cowboy were dismissed.

HE MOVED THE Rover to the employee lot—a dusty strip tucked out of sight around the corner of the house—and brought in his bags. His temporary quarters were a cramped closet near the wide white kitchen, and Vincent dropped everything on the too-small bed, unopened. No need for Alan, or anyone else for that matter, to see his supplies.

The tour of the house was irritating as all fuck, blind spots everywhere scratching and scraping at his nerves. He had the basic layout from guesswork; it was faintly comforting that there were few surprises. Looked like the kid was a boy, from the toy vehicles and blue all over his bedroom. On the other side of a vast playroom was a white-painted door, and Alan's eyebrows twitched twice as he pointed it out, the watch on his wrist glittering even though the face was turned to the inside of his wrist. "That's the nanny's room. Miss Halperin. She's . . ." A low whistle, another eyebrow-raise.

Vincent remembered a comedy show about a nanny with a high, broad accent a long time ago, but that probably wasn't what the man was referring to. "Trouble?"

"Only to your fuckin' pants, man." Alan laughed, the sound falling dead against carpet patterned with roads for toy cars to zoom along. "But the kid likes her. She's lasted six months, and el señor pays through the nose. She's good."

Vincent nodded to show he'd heard. He wasn't here to be friendly, just to loom in the background. *Halperin.* He filed the name away.

Probably a no-nonsense battle-axe who could give drill sergeants a run for their money. Wasn't there also a reality show about a British nanny? "What's the kid's name?"

"Eduardo." Alan's face didn't change. The kid was probably a nonentity to him.

Interesting. Vincent nodded again. "Okay." There was no reason to peek in the nanny's room, especially if she was the battle-axe type. Marquez wouldn't let anyone who couldn't pass a background check near his son; to that kind of guy, male offspring were ego reflections and consequently smother-guarded.

"It's the girl's day off, so the kid's with Emilia—that's the cook." Alan's good humor stayed solid, and he beckoned Vince back out into the hall. "You'll see her tomorrow at the party. It starts at six, social affair, keeping up with the neighbors, that sort of shit. You got anything you need to get?"

Please. I'm not an amateur. "Nope." Vincent kept his expression nice and bland, the wall you gave an officer just looking to hand out a disagreeable duty. "I brought everything."

"All right. I'll get back to work." The other man gave one last lingering glance in the direction of the nanny's room before sweeping the playroom's door mostly closed. "You just do what you gotta to set up. Stay out of el señor's office and the west hall, okay? He don't like anyone near his bedroom."

Who did? "Ten-four."

"Good deal, man." Another handshake, firm but not overcompensating, and Alan was gone.

Vincent made his way back to the empty kitchen, and from there it was easy to find his room, everything right where he left it. The window was tiny, and barred—maybe a cat could wriggle through, but he wouldn't bet on it. The bathroom was nothing fancy either—just washstand, mirror, and shitter. He could sponge-bathe, or use the employee locker room. Maybe the señor let the help use the pool, if they asked with cap in hand and toes digging into the floor.

After checking the walls, more out of habit than any real desire to find out if they were going to watch him piss, he folded himself down on the bed. A thin mattress. Not the worst he'd slept on. It all looked pretty standard.

A party full of rich fucks worried about keeping up with the Joneses, then babysitting a woman and a kid. It would keep him occupied for a little while, then he'd go back to Klemp and ask for something a little more active. Just to keep himself in shape, take the edge off—and Klemperer's commission for finding good help wasn't an apology for getting the man shot in the leg, but it could stand in for one.

It was a ricochet, nobody's fault, but when you were in command the buck didn't just stop with you, it rabbit-punched you in the balls.

Vince stared at the white popcorn ceiling for a half-hour or so, his nerves twitching every once in a while. Then it was time to get up and go over the house again, just to keep himself occupied.

Brooding about whether he was going to be permanently out to pasture wasn't going to do him any good.

The Wrong Thought

DINNER WAS ROAST beef, herbed new potatoes, salad, fresh bread, and tension. A faint breeze packed with the flat iron tang of sprinkler water slipped between the columns; despite late-evening heat, the short, covered gallery was a nicer place to eat than the vast, chilly dining room. The chairs were old, heavy wood glowing with beeswax, and citronella candles burned in blown-glass holders. Spiny yucca plants marched along the lawn side of the colonnade, and the two carafes—red wine, white wine—were somber jewels in the dusk.

As usual, all the benefits of getting a massage on her day off evaporated when Eddie went pale, staring at his plate, and his father speared another strip of tender, medium-rare cow corpse.

"Eat it." Holding his fork and steak knife Continental-style, wide-shouldered Mr. Marquez studied his son, and the glob of green-white paste he'd just put on the boy's square cobalt-blue plate.

Cara inhaled, deep and soft, trying to find her calm again and curling her toes in the strappy sandals she'd picked up at Carzano's Shoes for a song. Dressing for dinner was *not* part of the deal, but the wide-legged linen trousers and sleeveless top were slightly formal in honor of her day off. "Horseradish isn't good for him." She reached for her wineglass, took a decorous sip. Usually, she and Eddie ate with Emilia in the kitchen. Every once in a while, though, Dear Old Dad got yet another burr in his saddle about turning Eddie into a miniature version of himself, and Cara was invited to the show.

Maybe it didn't feel like a victory unless he had another adult there to witness it.

Mr. Marquez's square, poreless cheeks glistened; Cara had no idea what his 'business' entailed and didn't *want* to know. Whatever it was, it not only covered her own pay as well as the agency fee, but also his gray suit jacket—worth more than a month of said take-home pay—too. Even his shirts were flown in from a tailor in Hong Kong. "When I was his age, I was eating habañeros whole."

"Well, you didn't know any better." She could probably email the agency and get them to ask for yet another raise. That was covered in the contract. Maybe he'd fire her this time, and she could be done with the whole thing. It wouldn't even be her fault.

Except her stupid conscience would bite her if she left Eddie to his father's not-so-tender unmercies.

Mr. Marquez laughed, but his hazel eyes had turned cold; he dabbed at his sculpted lips with a snow-white napkin. "You gonna tell me what to do with my own son?"

"That's my job, sir." Cara met his gaze squarely. So far, working retail had prepared her better for this profession than any college courses. She should have gone for an associate's in psychology instead of her BFA. Unscented massage oil lingered on her skin, and the whole blessed hour of silence while she was under the therapist's hands had been the high point of the week. "The one you hired me for."

"Look at that." Mr. Marquez's grin, full of pearly, expensively reworked teeth, glittered. He picked up his silverware again, and Eddie glanced at Cara, the whites of his eyes like a frightened horse's. "You think you're his mama, huh?"

Eddie's mother had apparently died in a car accident; every time she was mentioned, Eddie's eyes got round. He wasn't squirming yet, just staring miserably at his plate and the glob of horseradish he could already tell he wouldn't like but might be forced to sample.

Unless she could do something about it.

"Sir." Cara set her own silverware down, gently. *If this is dick-measuring, amigo, mine's still bigger.* The right tone was firm but not combative, demure but not submissive, just like dealing with a fishbone-thin debutante who insisted she didn't need a receipt to exchange an expensive handbag. "When I took this position, you specifically requested that I be truthful with you about your son. Has that changed?"

"No." Her employer leaned back in his chair a little, ceding at least part of the battlefield. "Fine, fine. Don't eat it, Eddie. *La Chacha* thinks it's bad for you."

At least it was only a *faintly* pejorative term, the way he said it. Cara considered reaching for her wineglass again. It probably wasn't a good idea, but good Lord, was it ever tempting. Especially if she dumped it all over this jackass and his expensive shirts.

Would *that* be enough to get her fired? Possibly. It would certainly give the little boy a good memory to hang onto. Eddie sawed at his own roast beef, his shoulders hunching. He didn't look at her, since any grateful glance might set his father off again.

"Sit up straight," Mr. Marquez snapped. "Listen, señorita Cara. Alan told you about the party?"

"He mentioned you'd be having another one, yes." She knew better than to think the man had forgotten her small victory. He might make Eddie pay for it later, but at least the kid could eat in peace for a few minutes. "He also said you're going on a trip right after."

"Business." Thank God he didn't invite her along this time. *That* had been uncomfortable, but at least she'd had an iron-clad out. They covered it in the agency materials—a list of do's and don'ts, straight from the fifties. Penalties for what they called *improper behavior*, blaming the woman like any good misogynist institution. "We'll be gone a couple weeks. There's new security for you, so be nice."

"Thank you for letting me know." *I'll try not to be a screaming harpy.* God, the wine looked good. The longing thought of bringing home a bottle of something to keep in her room just wouldn't go away during these dinners. "I'll keep Eddie up for your phone calls."

Mr. Marquez nodded, expansive now that she'd acknowledged his control of bedtimes, at least. "You got a pretty dress for the party?" He didn't outright leer, thank God, but often treated her like a vapid teenage daughter on babysitting duty instead of an adult woman paid very well to look after his kid.

Hopefully when he was finished eating and picked out a cigar, she and Eddie could escape. Getting the kid into the bathtub was a chore, but when his father had been at him, he didn't kick too hard.

Eddie was old enough to consider her an ally. And Marquez was at least *interested* in his son. Neglect could wreak an entirely different sort of havoc on a kid.

The yucca rustled, and the good green smell of afternoon-clipped grass mixed with the beef and the wine's acid tang. "Nothing designer." A diplomatic answer—her grandmother would be proud of Cara not letting her mouth run, for once. Gemma Halperin had despaired of her daughter's only child ever learning to refrain from smarting off. "I think Eddie and I will have dinner early that night, and stay out of the way. Unless you want him to greet your guests." In other words, she was offering him another victory, to make up for the horseradish.

Sometimes she thought her real job was managing the father, not the kid. Jeanie said that was par for the course; she was on her third rotation. At least the twins' parents were actively involved with their spawn too, instead of alternately neglectful and smothering.

"If he's a good boy." Mr. Marquez dipped half a tiny potato into melted, herb-flecked butter, chewed with relish. His pinky ring glittered. "Eat up, Eduardo. Get strong."

The boy hunched even further, but he managed to get down a respectable portion of his dinner. Cara restrained herself from reaching for her wineglass again, and decided she'd lost her appetite. At least the man didn't badger *her* into eating.

Although it might also be temporarily and deeply satisfying to stab him with a fork. Contemplating that made her smile, and she nursed her waterglass until Emilia brought out the humidor for the señor to choose his after-dinner cigar.

Finally free, Cara ushered Eddie away for his bath.

HER OUTSIDE YOGA mat, thicker than her inside one, dangled like a sausage from its strap as Cara stepped through the pool gate, its familiar groan-creak-squeak a reminder that the worst of the day was now behind her. Or so she thought, until she spotted a dark blot on one of the cedar chairs.

Oh, for fuck's sake.

It was Alan, settled in for the evening with his boots up, a sweating Corona balanced on one armrest, and his hat lying on the slat table next to the chair.

Even at rest, the man was a goddamn cliché.

Cara could, she supposed, turn around and take her mat to the playroom. Of course, there was the security camera in the inner corner, and the thought of him sitting in the office watching her was just as unpalatable. She might as well stick to her usual routine and be comfortable. At least she could make sure her ass didn't point in Alan's direction, and rob him of *that* much.

Unrolling her mat made half the tension flee, and for the next half hour, she didn't really have to think. Mountain pose. Side bends. Forward bend. Downward dog. Low lunge. Warrior. Her usual routine, nothing fancy, breathing deep and letting the day settle. Sometimes Eddie wanted her to teach him stretches in the playroom, and his giggles at some of the names were sweetly amusing. The urge to grab and hug him was ever-present during those sessions.

Even here, the pad yielding between concrete and her pressing limbs, the past could slip in.

Fibroids, the doctor had said, her graying hair pulled tightly back and the stethoscope in her breast pocket glinting evilly. *Ten to twenty-five percent of known pregnancies end in . . .*

That word. That horrible, hateful word. The blood, the pain, and the cramping, all rolled up into three hurtful syllables. Cara pressed her palms down, braced herself, and tried not to think.

A headstand had to *be*, not *do*.

Kick up. Balance found in the core, legs straight like a diver's, the world upside-down, her head pounding and her arms trembling. Her hair, a loose braid, hung twitching like a pendulum. The first time she'd done this, what a rush—propped against a wall, red-faced and sweating, and having no idea a few months later she would be in a hospital bed bleeding, everything gone on a flood of reddish clots.

And her ex-husband Ben's familiar stubble-rough face, pale and drawn. *It's actually kind of a relief* . . .

That was the absolute wrong thought to have. Her left elbow folded; she managed to get her foot down so she only sprawled onto her left side instead of cracking her head on poolside concrete. "*Fuck*," she barked, and rolled, pushing herself up on numb hands.

"Hey." Alan, hurriedly bouncing up from his chair, almost knocked over his half-empty beer. "Damn. You okay?"

No. "Yeah." She shook the muffled ringing out of her ears, lunging upright. If he tried to 'help' her, she was going to kick him in the shins. "Just my pride." Why did she have to fall over where *he* could see? And her day had been going so well before dinner.

But that was life. You never could tell when something with sandpaper skin and triangular teeth was lurking below the surface of your daily routine, its dorsal fin hidden but its tail working as it came for you like an express train.

"That's some serious shit." He stopped, a decent distance away for once. It was a goddamn miracle. "You sure you're okay? I thought you were gonna stay there all night."

"I'm *fine*. Thank you." Cara settled back on her mat, sweat mixing with leftover massage oil. Maybe he was honestly concerned; now she felt slightly guilty for her immediate deep dislike of the man, no matter how hard he worked to justify it in other ways.

I know I'm a bitch. It's not news. She settled into staff pose, wincing. Maybe she should lay off the headstands for a while.

"That's pretty badass. Just hanging out upside down." Alan was now a shadow-blot in the dusk, outlined by glimmers off the pool as the floodlights began to switch on across the yard.

Cara leaned forward, grabbing her feet. She was going to bruise and stiffen up like nobody's business. "You should take up yoga," she said into her knees. "It does everyone good." A shower and some ibuprofen would help, and maybe Eddie wouldn't have the screamies again tonight.

She could hope.

"If it's spandex, I ain't interested." Alan ambled back to his chair.

Cara decided enough was enough, rolled up her mat, and padded inside without wishing him a good night *or* good luck.

It wasn't until she got in the shower that she realized her elbow was bleeding, and the side of her knee, too.

Great.

Play the Game

ALWAYS THE SAME dream, of course—not the mission that had bitten Klemp's leg, but one of the first he'd ever been on before the classified shit started. The glare, the sudden crumple-sodden thump *under the front left bumper, the weightlessness as the Humvee lifted like it intended to fly, the same stomach-flipping as the vehicle was grabbed by the iron hand of gravity and smacked back to earth, half torn open, shrapnel peppering the sand and pinging off sunbaked rocks. Sticky blood in his eyes, the strap of his helmet a python's squeeze against his jaw—and his fingertips outstretched, unable to reach the rifle, the sick sinking knowledge of exposure as he struggled inside what had been an armored vehicle but was now only a burst tin can.*

Then the screaming started, and the worst thing was, Vince wasn't sure if it was his own or Lewandoski's, because the kid was going to die half-crushed and wailing and there was nothing anyone could do, not even his squad leader—

FOR A FEW MOMENTS, waking in a room only a little bigger than a coffin, he had no idea where he was.

It was the hush that did it. This wasn't a tent or dormitory full of snoring, farting soldiers, no chatter of faraway small arms or bigger bursts of mortars as the sleepless decided to have some fun, no shouts, running feet, or running engines. And yet for an awful, terrifying, vertiginous instant he was back in the desert again, the skin-prickling silence of *shit's about to go down* rousing every nerve to singing, taut alertness.

Then he sagged, muscles gone liquid and bones buzzing with relief. He'd only been dreaming of the filth and the smell and the radio chatter. The need to move tautened like a puppet's string, and Vincent found himself sitting bolt-upright, reaching for the gun on the nightstand. Cool, heavy metal jolted him fully awake and he froze, pupils stretching wide to take in every available shred of light, his damp skin exquisitely sensitive to any stray breath of air. Tossing, turning, wrestling with sweat-soaked sheets—he could have stayed in his safe, utilitarian apartment, really, and had the same experience.

The white-painted room was dark and breathlessly still even with air conditioning. Vincent strained his ears—that must have been what awakened him, the soft subtle unsound of other people moving in the same structure. There was a clink and a faint gurgling, too—a coffee-maker, which meant the cook was up.

He set the gun down and checked his watch. Five a.m., not bad. If he was in the field he'd sleep like a baby whenever he could snatch a few consecutive empty minutes, but out here, the dreams were to be expected.

It didn't make them any easier to endure, but it helped to know he wouldn't have to deal with them again until after another full day's trudge through consciousness.

A few minutes later, cleaned up and lightly armed, Vince stepped into the kitchen's clean fluorescent glare, rubbing at his eyes with callused fingertips. The coffeemaker was burbling away, but there was no sign of the heretofore invisible cook. Or anyone else, really. The patio door was ajar, and the keypad next to it held a small, flashing green light. A heavy, chill-wet predawn breeze tiptoed through, and when Vince stepped outside it was like plunging into a tepid bath.

The desert got cold at night, and its dry breath was far different than AC.

The sprinklers were on, chugging away with single-minded intensity; he edged around the patio, keeping to the shadows. When he reached a corner he stopped, replaying what he remembered of the layout. There should be the bigger patio, the swimming pool, the end of a long colonnaded gallery just visible past it, and violently green lawn sloping down to the shrubbery around the estate's walls.

When he edged past the corner, he found out he was right, as usual.

Still, it was good to play the game. He was about to turn away, but a flicker of motion caught his gaze.

A slim woman with a messy, dark high-pulled chignon perched on a yoga mat near the pool, arms over her head. She bent, supple as a stem, and hugged her legs, straightened halfway, then placed her palms flat and stepped back, hips high, stretching with a visible wince. Her skin glowed in the strengthening grey light. A pale cotton tank top clung to her upper half, and loose workout pants fluttered as she brought her right foot up near her right hand, knee bent, and stretched some more.

It had to be the nanny. Suddenly Alan's eyebrow-waggling made sense. Vince couldn't see her face, but she moved with fluid grace, and the body was enough to give a man a few pleasant thoughts. He didn't like them too skinny, and she had a beautiful curve to her hips.

Vincent stood, sunk in shadow, and watched her move. She flowed from one pose to the next with controlled authority, and he almost flinched when she turned to face the other way on her mat. If he moved, she might have seen him in the strengthening dawn—except her eyes were closed as she breathed, ribs flaring under thin cotton and her breasts lifting slightly each time.

He stared, mesmerized, his lungs burning. High cheekbones, winged dark eyebrows, a sweet mouth slightly open as if she'd just been kissed—oh, it was so she could breathe properly, but he could imagine, couldn't he?

Damn. Vincent almost envied the kid, having that vision in front of him all the time.

A sudden cessation of noise—the sprinklers, having fulfilled their duty, were throttled—almost drove him into a crouch. She didn't seem to notice, turning away and moving into another series of poses, each one held for a bare few seconds. It wasn't fair for a woman to do that, especially when her hair was coming loose and falling in thick dark almost-curls, probably softer than silk and just begging for a man's fingers to comb, gather a handful, watch them slip away.

Vincent eased back, toes down first, rolling through the movement silently. The silence was profound, except for a clanking clatter from the open kitchen door behind him. He realized he was still sweating, and for the first time since he'd come home, his body was taking an interest in something other than eating, fighting, or getting back into fatigues.

Calm down, soldier. Just get down easy and take five. Hell, take ten. Just don't embarrass yourself.

He shook out his hands, blinked, and turned as if on parade, stalking back for the irregular slice of light that was the open kitchen door.

It was going to be a busy day.

Safe Haven

EVERY PARTY THE world over, from college shindig to business wheel-greaser, was the same. Someone would invariably show up early and demand to be amused, someone would arrive in high dudgeon looking for a fight, and someone would breeze through the door in dramatically late fashion expecting to be noticed. Whether it was a preschooler's birthday bash or a high-end adult soirée, there were certain inevitable benchmarks, and so far Cara hadn't been disappointed *or* surprised.

At least this wasn't one of Marquez's poker nights. She suspected those were where the real "business" happened; these regular shindigs were just to keep his finger on the pulse of the other nouveau riche—legitimately or otherwise—in the area. All of them were angling for the right country club invitation, and Cara wished them luck.

The house throbbed with inoffensive easy-listening music from very expensive hidden speakers while champagne poured into flutes to lubricate social interaction. Emilia's kitchen was a hive of activity, caterers performing various tasks under her eagle eye, and the extra security staff lurked in corners and at entrances, their earbuds in and their faux-military haircuts ready, a sprinkling of watchfulness among the well-dressed, already slightly inebriated crowd doing its best to both impress each other and ignore "the help."

Cara's own backless Yanka Martina dress with its slick silver sheen like wet scales turned her into a prospective fellow guest, though her lack of expensive skincare put her firmly in "the help" category. In short, she was neither beast nor fish nor good red herring, as Grandma Gemma would say; those who knew Marquez more than by sight saw Eddie clinging to her hand and smirked. At least the dress had long sleeves to cover the scrape on her elbow, a hem low enough to cover her knees, and a very modest draped neckline; her lack of updo provided one more indication of her in-between status. And with her hair halfway down, the backless gown wasn't an invitation, just her own private joke.

After all, yoga gave you great muscle definition, especially an hour twice daily when you had no social life to speak of. She was just attractive enough to avoid being mocked, which was fine by her.

Eddie, his hair wet-combed into submission and his tiny tailored suit only mildly uncomfortable—to judge by his resigned expression—clung to her hand except when forced to greet some of the guests. His father's expansive comments whenever they were in range and the men who bent to pinch Eddie's cheek and call him *a spitting image* had exactly the same effect as a wire brush on varnished wood.

Cara had to suppress an entirely uncharacteristic desire to snatch a few by their expensive suit-fronts and hiss *Back off, for God's sake, he's a human being, not livestock*. How would any of *them* like being pinched and prodded?

The women were slightly better, cooing about how cute he was and calling him *young man*. Eddie's shy smile in response provoked no few of them to pronounce him a little heartbreaker, and Cara's own grin was half-embarrassed in its pride—she was, after all, only the nanny—but still absolutely genuine.

Eddie was allowed to stay up a half-hour past his bedtime, and Cara almost managed to vanish unremarked with him at the appointed hour. Her feet hurt from the point-toe diamanté heels she rarely had occasion to wear and her lower back was protesting again.

Later, she'd figure the precipitating event was her burst of relief when it was finally time to withdraw, guiding Eddie towards the hall that would take them to the kitchen. At least *that* was a safe haven, even if jammed to the gills with caterers, but the entrance was blocked by a knot of laughing socialites.

And even more unfortunately, they were caught halfway to the kitchen by a very drunk woman in a silver-dripping twenties-style flapper dress and a short pixie-cap of inky hair, who just *had* to coo over a very uncomfortable Eddie in broken Spanglish. Cara smiled and nodded, knowing she shouldn't have let herself feel any relief until it was all over, so to speak. The instant Eddie cast her a mute, appealing glance—the look he'd learned not to use on his father, because the señor saw it as weakness—Cara gave a brisk, "Very sorry, we have to go, his father's orders." She had to almost pry the woman's fingers from Eddie's arm, and the urge to give a savage twist surprised her.

"Shut up," the woman hissed, her face contorting. "You wore my dress."

Oh, for God's sake. Cara straightened. She'd spent a summer cocktail waitressing in college, and it was the instinct from that strange, smelly, subterranean time that squared her shoulders and brought her chin up.

"Back *off*," she whisper-hissed in return, and pulled Eddie into her hip. "Ma'am."

"Ma'am?" Thankfully, one of the new security goons—a tall chunk of brick shithouse with cropped-close dark hair and the type of stubble that rarely went away even when a man shaved twice daily—was looming close, his black suit good but not nearly as good as a guest's. He even had the flat professional stare Alan sometimes wore, though he didn't raise her hackles the way Dracula Cowboy did. "Everything all right here?" He aimed the question right between them, a good hard volleyball serve.

The drunk woman giggled, suddenly coquettish with the appearance of a male, and Cara didn't wait to thank her deliverer. She simply hustled Eddie past, even though that meant they had to go at an angle, taking them through the smallest living room. Still, that would get them past the fraying knot of socialites to the playroom hall, and from there it was smooth sailing, even if the señor glimpsed them from a knot of casually clad businessmen glowing with the arrogant gloss of real money.

That was a change. Maybe Marquez was moving up in the food chain. The boss stared at Cara and her charge, a long considering look.

That's weird. But she didn't stop until she swept the playroom door closed behind them, heaving a half-unconscious sigh. Eddie's chest flickered with deep, nervous breaths and he plucked at his little suit jacket over and over, not quite daring to take it off yet. His forehead was damp and his big dark eyes glimmered.

"I thought she was gonna eat me," he muttered.

Not a bad estimation of the situation, small fry. "Nope." Cara swallowed an entirely inappropriate laugh. "Not with me around, Ed. Let's get you out of that monkey suit."

"Monkey suit." His face scrunched up, and he did a passably good imitation of a simian tree-swinger.

This time laughter boiled out of her, colored deep wine-red with relief as she bent to unbutton his jacket. In short order he was in his pajamas, and from the looks of it, *extremely* glad the operation didn't entail another bath.

He didn't even protest when she tucked him into his race car bed, though he did fix her with his best mournful look. "Can I have the window open?" Not content to plead, he also blinked owlishly, his particular version of batting his lashes, unfairly thick and long as some boys were blessed with. "Please?"

"No deal, kiddo." Cara stretched, her fists pressing into her lower back once more. "Let's give the air-conditioner the night off."

"But I can't breathe with it closed." His lower lip quivered slightly, and his dark eyes glimmered.

"You're doing just fine right now." Something bothered her, and she wanted a few moments' peace to figure it out.

"Well, I'm *hungry.*" Eddie's mobile face scrunched up again, and his hair had begun to shake free of the wet comb-slicking. His curls were a constant source of vexation to Mr. Marquez, but Cara thought they suited the kid really well.

"You do realize you'd have to brush your teeth again if I brought you a snack, right?" Cara pressed her lips together, shaking out her hands and bending to smooth the covers over him. He'd kick them off as soon as he fell asleep, but it was comforting to be tucked in—or so she hoped. "Nice try, though."

"Okay, okay." He snuggled back down, content now that the world had assumed its old familiar routine and dimensions. Ritual was comforting when you weren't even half the size of everyone around you. "Kiss?"

"I can do that." She pressed her lips to his damp forehead, and the pain went through her chest again. Sometimes it was almost sweet, but this time it had claws.

It wasn't until she dropped onto her own narrow bed, working the damn diamanté shoes off with a relieved sigh, that she realized what was bothering her so much.

Mr. Marquez, in the middle of the circle of bankers, had looked angry. *Very* angry. Still urbane, still smiling, but she knew that glitter in his hazel eyes; the faint, almost imperceptible twitch in one of his almost-square cheeks also spoke volumes. Especially when you'd sat at a dinner table with the man and listened to him try to take apart his child emotionally.

Eddie was going to need therapy when he got older, and Cara couldn't do a damn thing about it.

What bothered her most was seeing that look on her employer in the middle of a party, surrounded by adults. It was one thing for a petty tyrant to show a kid and an employee his displeasure. It was another thing entirely when he was among his so-called peers, although if they were like the pixie in the silver dress, maybe they were too drunk or self-centered to notice. In any case, it was none of her concern; the agency practically papered its workers with NDAs. Even if she *did* know what business Roderigo Marquez was in, she couldn't do anything about it, and that was just fine with her.

Now Cara realized what else was bothering her. In the den, his arms folded, Alan had stood near a massive, round gas-insert fireplace sheathed with glass, and his smirk was familiar. For once, though, he hadn't been looking at her.

No, he'd been looking at señor Marquez.

Not your job, Cara told herself, and tossed the damn shoes approx.-imately in the direction of the closet. Tonight's yoga practice was going to have to be next to her bed.

Great.

STRETCHED OUT and pleasantly tired, propped on her pillows with a glossy architecture magazine upon her knees, Cara listened to the party and wiggled her toes, glad to be out of the dress—even though it was pretty—and even gladder to be out of her shoes. The guests probably thought they were having fun, judging from the blur and buzz of voices, but she'd take her own room and relative quiet any day.

Eddie would probably have called it unfair, but *her* window was wide open, mostly because her room overheated with the door closed and she might as well get a breath or two of dry desert breeze if she was going to read in bed. When she turned the light out, she could close the window and open her door; air-conditioning from the playroom would help her sleep.

Cara yawned, paging through a spread on a particular Frank Lloyd Wright she'd seen a million times before, and her stomach growled. Now she felt a little guilty for putting Eddie to bed without at least a snack, and she sighed, setting the magazine aside and stretching luxuriously.

She could just get a glass of water from the bathroom sink and settle to sleep, but her conscience pinched again. If he was still awake, she'd grab something from the kitchen for them both.

Fortunately, she didn't have to wriggle back into the dress. Her social duties were done for the night; as long as she stayed out of the party areas, she'd go unremarked. She did slide a long sleeveless linen robe over her tank top and pajama pants, a gesture for modesty she couldn't wait to slip out of once she was safely back in her room.

Eddie was on his back, deeply asleep, both arms flung wide and his blankets kicked into a mess. Cara shook her head and padded out into the hall.

One look at the hallway's living-room end convinced her she had to find another route. She took a hard left, heading down a few steps and through an almost invisible employee door. It was no warmer outside than it had been in her room, but sweat prickled under her arms and behind her knees, not to mention on her neck under heavy unbound hair.

It was a lovely night, a promise of autumn crispness in the distance, and there was a breath of chlorine as well as giggling and several splashes from the pool. Someone was enjoying that, at least.

She kept to the shadows, edging along a concrete walkway mostly neglected by the landscapers, dried leaves crunching faintly under her slippers.

Later, she would wonder what might have happened if she hadn't checked on Eddie, or if she'd chosen to just drink a glass of water instead of milk. As it was, she was about to round the corner and pass the giant picture-window before joining up with the patio outside the kitchen door when she heard a familiar voice.

"What's the fuckin' problem?" Alan growled.

Cara froze, her hair swinging as she glanced wildly around. She was behind a hedge of tough, spiny succulents, and the lights—every blessed one turned on for the party, the entire estate a network of jeweled stars—didn't reach this tiny corner. Where exactly was he?

"It's a simple job," the head of Marquez's security continued, obviously trying to keep his voice down but unable to. It sounded like he was on the phone. Now she could see an indistinct Alan-shape through the spiny foliage. He'd chosen a good spot not to be overheard, and his outline looked monstrous for a moment before she realized he was plugging one ear in order to hear better through the one he had the phone clasped to. "Are you telling me it's beyond you?"

Oh, for God's sake. She thought of backing up, immediately discarded the notion. She'd probably run into the bushes. Her cheeks were hot, an automatic guilty flush—the natural consequence of having a conscience, even if you were doing nothing wrong. It was like waiting for your debit card to be approved at the grocer's even when you knew you had plenty of money to cover the total.

"Good." Alan sounded satisfied, or at least, a little less pissed off. "Now remember, not a scratch on the big package. The little one will make 'er easier to handle."

A soft breeze freighted with sage, mesquite, and sand rattled the bushes, pushing against the house like a cat stropping a beloved human's legs. Cara's lungs turned heavy; she held her breath.

"So?" Alan listened for a few moments, then made a short, plosive noise of irritation. "I don't care how you do it, just get it done in time. We're on a schedule here, asshole."

With that, he hung up, but he didn't move. Instead, he stood with his back to her, and Cara found herself pressing her fingertips against her lips. *Don't move. God, I don't like this guy.* He was no more than a minor annoyance of the type any reasonably attractive woman had to deal with on a daily basis, but still, something about him raised the hairs on her nape.

It was getting worse the longer she stayed. Maybe she should invent a boyfriend—this kind of man didn't back off until he thought you were a bigger dick's property.

"Coming along fine," Alan said, softly, musingly. For a moment she thought he was on another call, but he was just talking to himself. And then, blessedly, he moved away, slipping the phone back into his pocket and turning left—checking the grounds, probably—instead of right, towards the kitchen. He vanished like a bad dream.

Cara's breath whooshed out and she sagged gratefully, wondering if she was still hungry enough to risk continuing. It was ridiculous to stand out in the night, sweating and shaking, just because she'd overheard a phone conversation.

Later, she would think maybe she'd somehow known, or should have suspected. But at the time she just shook her head, turned on slightly unsteady legs, and shuffled back to find another way to the kitchen.

Strange Things

THAT'S WHY HE'S paying cash, Vincent realized, watching Marquez work the room. Klemp would say the man was slick as gooseshit; most of his employees and about half the guests probably had no idea he was anything other than a nouveau riche looking to break into the country club set by hook, crook, or overstretched credit.

The other half of the guests were . . .interesting. *Look at a man's shoes,* Vince's dad used to say, *and they'll tell you everything you need to know.* Oh, plenty of them wore dressy polished numbers, but it was the thick Vibram soles that gave them away. These were men ready to move at less than a moment's notice, sort of like Vince himself. Then there was the redheaded fellow with two broad-shouldered "friends" who were carrying one or two knives they shouldn't.

Again, like Vince himself.

Not to mention the woman with a thin white scar along her jawline, her navy silk pantsuit understated in the way only true wealth could manage and the deference each guest paid her—civilian or otherwise—thought-provoking in the extreme. Navy Suit's dark, liquid eyes roamed the room in precisely calculated arcs, and her security was both unobtrusive and well-heeled, as well as fully armed.

Which would have given Vincent a bad feeling about the whole thing, if he hadn't caught one of said security's eye and received the slight nod that said *I see you, but we're not here for you.*

Good enough.

It looked, in short, like there was a fair amount of actual business being transacted, if the group around the señor—falling silent whenever a civilian wandered too close—was any indication.

The only truly odd note was the nanny, holding the hand of a baby-bellied boy with Marquez's eyes, dimpled hands, and a crop of curls only held down by sheer willpower and the application of a wet comb. She didn't ever turn loose of the kid, and something about the way he clung to her spoke of real affection.

Was she oblivious to that, or to the likely sources of her employer's wealth? It was an open question.

There was a moment of trouble when one of the true civilians in a similarly glittering dress buttonholed the nanny-and-kid duo, and Vince moved in without thinking—they were, after all, his packages, even if he hadn't been introduced. After a few murmured words the drunken bitch backed off, but all Vincent received for his pains was a single glance from the nanny's wide dark eyes, slotting him into a category—*the help* or maybe even *hired goon*—before she hustled the kid in a different direction and disappeared into a hall that would take them to the playroom.

He returned to his post, telling himself it was only natural that he'd move in to make initial contact. Still, he wasn't really seeing the party, guests ebbing and flowing as utterly forgettable music—more like noise pollution, he'd even take thrash metal over this bullshit easy listening—echoed from hidden speakers.

No, what Vincent was seeing was wide dark eyes and wavy almost-black hair pulled back in an artistically messy half-braid that left most of its mass tumbling down her back. High cheekbones and a sharp nose, a full mouth touched only with the barest hint of gloss. That mouth was dangerous, or it would have been if it relaxed from the tense, small, apologetic smile of a woman who understood very well she was allowed to the party only on sufferance. It was a shame, because her dress had the same rainbow-silver sheen as a pigeon's throat, and it clung to curves that begged for exploration. Even the slim column of her neck shouted silent reserve, but those big eyes had flashed a warning that needed no translation at the drunk woman.

Maybe she actually cared about the kid. It wouldn't be the first time a nanny got attached; that was a hazard of the job, like high-speed lead poisoning and bad nerves were a hazard of his.

It didn't matter what side of the law Marquez was on. He was paying, and that was all Vince cared about.

Or not quite. If the guy was what he suspected—import-export, so to speak, or something a little more refined—it meant there was a chance of action.

Vincent's stomach settled all at once, and the faint ghost of sweat under his arms cooled rapidly.

"Enjoying the party?" It was Alan, one half of his mouth curved up in a wolfish smile. His suit was exactly the same kind as Vince's own, maybe even with one or two tailored bits to hide a surprise. He'd lost the hat though his hair still remembered it, but he hadn't ditched the belt buckle or the shiny toecaps on his high-end cowboy boots.

Two weeks in basic would iron this guy flat. It was an amusing thought. "Lots of liquor," Vince replied, *sotto voce.* It wouldn't do to insult the guests. "Anyone here got a bad temper?"

"Just me, man." Alan's grin didn't change, but his gaze flickered restlessly. "You seen the nanny and the kid? They were just here."

"Went that way a little bit ago." He indicated the hallway she'd vanished into, the little curly-headed boy in tow. He should have checked his watch when they withdrew, but he'd been . . .distracted? Was that the word? "Kind of late for a kid to be up."

Alan shrugged, and the motion didn't make his shoulder holster peep out to see what he was looking at. That was good tailoring. "She's probably tucking him in. Maybe she'll even come back."

"Maybe." Vincent studied the man. Did Alan actually sound hopeful? Looked like he had plans where the nanny was concerned, though Marquez didn't seem the type to like the help getting friendly with each other.

And the nanny looked too high-grade even for the man Alan obviously thought himself.

"We'll have to introduce you tomorrow. I was hoping to do it tonight, but el señor needs a lot of attention." In other words, Alan was the right-hand dude, and wanted everyone to know it.

"I think he's looking for you." Vince aimed for diplomacy and let his gaze drift over Alan's shoulder, as if caught by a gesture from the king of this little realm.

Marquez might even be good for other work, the kind the rest of Vince's team would be happy to take in order to sand their own edges down. If, that was, any of them, from Kemp on down to Jackson, were feeling the itch like he was.

He didn't know, and maybe he was thinking clearly for the first time in weeks because the not-knowing bothered him a little.

"Wouldn't be the first time," Alan said sourly, and turned away. He made it about halfway across the room before being caught by the pixie-cut woman in silver who had waylaid the nanny. Looked like she had a few complaints, and knew he was the man to take them to.

It was even halfway funny, so Vincent looked away. He stood his post, steered a few drunken guests away from the hall leading to the kitchen, and kept a weather eye out. The hours ticked by, his feet ached, and there was no trouble to speak of.

There also wasn't hide or hair of the nanny, and by two a.m., when the last of the civilians were bundled into their cars to be driven home and put to bed, he realized he'd been hoping to see her just as much as Alan had.

HE ALSO THOUGHT he'd have trouble dropping off, but he was gone as soon as his head hit the thin pillow. Which was the strangest thing of all.

Just the Help

LEAVING THE PARTY early was, like all good decisions, only visibly beneficial in retrospect, because it meant Cara achieved solid sleep. For once, Eddie didn't have night terrors—maybe he was too worn out from all the excitement—and she had nothing even approaching a nightmare either.

Which meant she was fresh as a daisy for the ritual goodbyes on the broad stone front steps before the massive front door, in bright morning sun that threatened to hammer the entire world flat, iron it smooth, and desiccate it for good measure.

"Little man." Mr. Marquez shook his head, patting Eddie's cheek with just a fraction more roughness than was strictly necessary, a lion velvet-pawing a cub. His suit's creases could have cut butter, ironed by his favorite dry cleaner, and his pinkie ring glittered. He wore extremely expensive aviator sunglasses, the mirrored lenses distorting his son's reflection. "You listen to *La Chacha* there. You go back to school soon."

"Yes, Pap—ah, Dad." Eddie smiled, his big dark eyes shining. The boy loved his father; it was beyond Cara how such a round, soft, small face couldn't immediately melt anyone's heart, but the señor didn't soften even a fraction. He tapped Eddie's cheek a little too hard once more, and Cara had to swallow a flare of acid, red-tinted anger.

Don't say anything. Don't get attached. A hot breeze played with her hair and mouthed the luxurious black SUV that would carry Mr. Marquez away on whatever business called. Alan stood by an open rear door, his hands respectfully crossed in front but his gaze fixed on her, his eyes gleaming under the brim of that dark, well-worn hat. It had to have some emotional value; he could well afford a new one.

Cara did her best to ignore the stare. Her entire body itched with heat; she longed to be inside with a glass of ice water and a good book. "I'll keep him up for your phone calls," she said, calmly enough. "And we'll work on his reading and spelling every day, like usual." Eddie was right on target for a first-grader, and when school started he was going to blow them out of the water. She couldn't wait to see his pride, even if it might mean her job was in jeopardy.

"Good, good." Now Marquez's gaze swung to her as he straightened and nodded towards one of the guards. "This is Vincent, Vincent Desmarais." He handled the name well, one romance language preparing the tongue for another. "He'll be looking after you."

It was the dark-haired, musclebound guy from last night, the fellow who'd made the drunk pixie back off. He loomed at the top of the stairs, his flat gaze roving the circular driveway and fountain, his hands clasped just like Alan's. She supposed they were trained to do that, in whatever factory turned out the men Marquez and his fellow rich folks hired for security. This morning Vincent was in jeans, T-shirt, and a hip-length leather jacket instead of a suit, and his boots were sensible sand-colored military lace-ups without fancy glittering toe-caps. His belt buckle was sensible too, instead of an advertisement.

It probably wasn't fair to compare him to Alan, but all she felt was relief at the prospect of a few days without Dracula Cowboy hanging around.

"We've met." Cara tried a smile and Eddie stepped close, leaning into her hip. He was doing that a lot lately. "Last night at the party. I'm Cara Halperin." She offered her right hand, but the man simply looked down at her from his perch two steps up.

Cara put her hand down, her smile fading, and turned back to the boss.

"Good, good." Marquez didn't look like he liked the idea of her meeting people at *his* parties, but what could he say? "Listen, you stay with the fellow, huh? If you leave the house—"

"—especially with Eddie, safety's the rule." Chapter and verse, and they'd gone over it at the agency, too. Varying your route home from any appointment, being aware of your surroundings, the whole nine yards. Not that many parents would pay a ransom for the nanny, but a kidnapped kid was a different matter entirely—and she suspected the bigger consideration might be the inconvenience to the important people paying for said nanny's services. Plus, there was only so much insurance the agency could carry, even with what it charged the parents. "Don't worry, sir. We'll go to the park, the library, and the mall, but that's about it."

"Good girl." Still, Marquez didn't smile. A line between his eyebrows promised trouble later, but hopefully not for Eddie. He was uncharacteristically distracted this fine morning. "Well, suppose we should go, eh?"

Yeah, get out of here. She couldn't wait to see the taillights, frankly; seeing Eddie lose that pinched expression would be best of all. "Business waits for no man." Her underarms and the hollows behind her knees prickled with sweat. It wouldn't have been so bad except for the sun bouncing off acres of concrete, gathering force and baking the driveway like a camping oven.

"*Sí, señorita.* The business never waits." He tousled Eddie's curls, gently for once—probably because he had to reach near her to do so—and turned briskly, striding for the car. Alan's chin tipped gently up and he stared past his employer, eyeing Cara like a matador with a particularly unresponsive toro.

She had a moment's worth of amusement imagining him in front of a *real* bull, and maybe he thought her smile was something else because he grinned back, a sudden sunny change from his usual saturnine self. He must've been using white strips, because his teeth all but glowed. He'd taken to getting his hair trimmed regularly, too.

It wasn't an improvement, as far as she was concerned.

"Wave goodbye, Eddie." She stroked the boy's head; he didn't duck away, just lifted a solemn hand. Car doors slammed, the engine roused, but the windows were so tinted she couldn't see if Marquez turned to look back.

Maybe he just didn't know how to show real affection. It was, she supposed, possible for a super-macho man who clawed his way up into money to miss that particular lesson. Probably was a help instead of a handicap, too.

Eddie stood very still as the cars—a sedan in front, the SUV in the middle, another black SUV following, a real cavalcade—skirted the fountain and turned onto the drive. Sunshine twinkled cheerfully off glass and metal, and Cara's ribs heaved with a deep involuntary sigh as the iron gate closed after the last set of ruby lights.

"Well, that's done." She half-turned, eyeing the new security guy. "Vincent, right?"

"Yes ma'am." He was watching the gate too, and his proud nose lifted a little. Maybe he didn't really want to be stuck with them, or maybe he was glad for an easy assignment. Either way, his expression was set like he smelled something faintly bad but was too polite to mention it. "Vincent Desmarais, ma'am." He handled the pronunciation differently, and she took careful note.

Everyone deserved to have their name said right. God knew even *hers* had been mispronounced more than once.

Desmarais was almost handsome in bright light, if you liked your boys broad in the beam and strong-jawed; his stubble was a stubborn bluish tint on planed cheeks. A tight, pained mouth, a buzzcut just this side of butch, and a high, very proud nose finished the picture of a man resigned to the inevitable, and he paid no further attention to her and Eddie than he would an unsolicited fruit basket.

Eddie tugged at her hand. "Can we go to the park?"

Oh, God, no. "It's a hot day, kiddo. Besides, you've still got your spelling worksheet to do this morning." She couldn't help but tousle his hair as well, but gently, and he tried to frown.

"Don't. I'm a big boy." As usual, once his father was gone Eddie was his usual talkative self again. He had his favorite green baseball shirt on, and his brand new high-tops with the flashing lights in the heels—armor, just like Cara's small silver hoop earrings.

"You certainly are." She eyed Vincent again. "I guess you're off duty, since we're not going anywhere."

"Never off duty." Three short, sharp words, and he didn't move when she edged past, Eddie peeking around her curiously. "Thanks."

Well, begrudging politeness was better than none. "All right." Cara gave him a wide berth, and Eddie's hand tightened on hers. "If you change your mind—"

"I won't," Vincent barked, but he followed her inside and shut the door, locking it with quick finger-flicks. "I'm just the help, ma'am. You don't have to be polite."

Believe me, I don't want to be. You're just getting the benefit of the doubt. She grabbed her patience with both hands, as Grandma Gemma would have said, and reached for a smile. "Well, I'm just the help too." The air-conditioning was an ice bath, and her sweat would dry rapidly, crinkling and itching.

"No you're *not*," Eddie said hotly, but she shushed him.

"Come on, let's go." That was about all the tact she had energy for, at least in Vincent's direction. "It's spelling time."

"I hate spelling." He twisted, still holding her hand, and glared at Vincent. "And I hate him, too."

"That's not nice, Eddie. Let's go." At least it was easier to redirect a kid than Alan. She tried an apologetic glance at the security guy, but he wasn't paying attention at all. He just moved to one side of the door and folded his arms, staring at the other end of the foyer.

Well, great. Cara swallowed an unwanted—from the looks of it—explanation, and hustled Eddie along.

BIG SPARE EMILIA, her braids crowning a face that could have come from an Aztec codex, chattered in Spanish and English with Eddie while Cara perched on her own stool at the counter, almost dizzy from the release of tension. Dinner was, for once, a pleasant affair; Emilia didn't quite comment on the señor's absence, but her eyes twinkled and she refilled both women's wineglasses twice. Cara's held white wine, Emilia's orange juice—*the alcohol, it makes me too sleepy*, she said.

I'll drink yours, Cara often replied, and both women always laughed. Once Eddie had been attended to, they talked about music—Emilia was a rabid live-rock and *corrida* fan, always going to one show or another with earplugs firmly in and a little notebook in hand for scribbling thoughts, impressions, and set lists. Every once in a while, she wrote reviews for a local free paper, too.

She had the feeling Emilia pitied her, locked in the house all the time, and at least part of the downloading about each and every live show was to give the poor gringa nanny a taste of excitement. It was a gift, and one Cara took gratefully.

Cara's good mood held all the way through bedtime; she read Eddie not three but *five* stories, including his favorite about a race car who had to learn the value of cooperation. For a kid with such a domineering father, Eddie certainly liked stories about sharing. Maybe it was a natural development.

Any day that good had to have a price tag attached; she should have known as much. The bill came due in the dead watches of the night when she sat straight up in her narrow bed, her hands clapped over her mouth to catch a scream as the same old dream returned—the blood, the cramping, the agonizing pain, and Ben's half-ashamed, half-grateful expression.

It's actually kind of a relief. . . And his expression as he watched her face, obviously expecting her to understand.

And Cara did, in that one blinding instant. He hadn't been ready, was what he meant; he hadn't been *prepared* for the changes a new arrival would bring. He'd probably expected her to agree, too, the way she always had with a man she was sure she loved.

Agreement went out the window when hacksaw cramps tore through you and a new life was spilled out on a tide of semisolid crimson. And really, Cara had only herself to blame. She'd known from the start that Ben, though gentle and intelligent, was weak.

Or if not weak, lazy, and that amounted to the same damn thing. Dried sweat was a crackglaze on her skin, and every muscle ached from both terror and stretching. She'd pushed herself in evening practice, probably as punishment for daring to have a decent time during dinner.

Trembling filled her to the brim, hot liquid in her bones instead of marrow. Her left hand dropped, pressing against the blankets over her lower belly, pushing in, knuckles digging, and she realized she was making a low, hurt noise.

Stop it. Just stop. It's over, it's done, you can't do anything about it now. Her silly, shaking body didn't know it, though, and wouldn't believe any calm rationality.

Finally the shuddering waves retreated, with a final vicious shake warning her they weren't done, just gathering strength for a new round. Cara spilled out of her bed, clutching her pillow in one weak hand, and left her room.

The playroom carpet scratched her bare feet, and she avoided stray Legos by mere chance. Eddie's window was slightly open—she hadn't done that, the kid must have snuck out of bed.

She didn't have the heart to even *think* a reprimand in his direction. Instead, she simply latched the window shut and lowered herself to the floor next to his red race car bed, letting out a silent sigh of relief as she settled.

His breathing was a soft, deep swell, a silent ocean. Eddie was on his back, arms flung wide and his chin up, mouth slightly open, and the slight reverberation of air through his nose wasn't quite a snore. It was soothing music, and her tension drained away.

She tucked the pillow under her head, turned on her side, and knew she'd be sore-stiff in the morning. But for the moment, the sound of someone else's breathing was a balm, and Cara dropped into dreamlessness.

Just before she did, though, she thought of Alan's bright, wide smile, as if they shared a secret. He couldn't know she'd heard him on the phone . . .but still, it unnerved her.

Just a little.

In Play

Complete Forgiveness

VINCENT WAS UP early for breakfast, and the tall, attractive cook—Emilia, he reminded himself, though he kept his manners on and called her *ma'am* by reflex—gave him a shy smile when he thanked her for breakfast eggs and bacon. He got the idea she didn't hear those words a lot. The coffee was too thin but at least it wasn't decaf, and the bacon was strong, smoky, and just crisp enough.

Another viciously hot day poured golden sunlight over every edge, and even the best air-conditioning would have a tough time keeping a greenhouse on wheels cool. The boxy black Volvo sedan set aside for the nanny's use would no doubt do its best, but leaving the car in any parking lot was going to mean coming back to an oven.

It wasn't that bad to drive, though. Heavy, dependable, and safe, even if it had little to no pickup—of course, you didn't want to give a nanny a sporty little number unless you were fucking her, and as much cash as Marquez was throwing around, it didn't look like he'd even put a deposit down on the girl.

Vincent couldn't quite figure out why he was so relieved to make *that* little deduction. It certainly couldn't have anything to do with the sky-blue maxi dress she wore, her bare shoulders probably saturated with sunscreen. Couldn't have anything to do with the fact that her mouth had relaxed and her large dark eyes were no longer quite so somber, either.

She wasn't any trouble, strapping the kid into his booster behind the driver's seat with only a single longing glance at the steering wheel. Looked like she knew the drill. Vince had to put his seat considerably back; he leaned over and made sure the front passenger one was brought all the way up. Her legs were long and lean, there was no reason for her to chew her own kneecaps back there.

"You'll want to take a right out of the gate," she said, and Vincent nodded. He'd looked up routes and alternates as soon as she'd informed him *Friday's library day, then we go to the park.*

"I know," he added, in case she didn't see the motion. "I've got it all up here, ma'am." A single tap at his temple with two fingertips, not quite a salute.

"He speaks," she said, softly, and turned to the kid, probably making a face because the little boy giggled.

Vincent's jaw set. *I just don't yammer when I have nothing to say, thanks.* He turned the key and hit the garage opener, his stomach gurgling once and settling as soon as it realized he was working again.

Even babysitting was better than nothing. A faint breath of her perfume—roses and an edge of spice—reached him over the good smell of expensive leather seats and the tang of sun protection on both her and the kid. It was the leather that surprised him; even if Marquez had an employee driving the Volvo around, it was still a nice car.

The big glass shell of the library was only twenty minutes away—practically nothing out here where you had to have a car even to go to the corner store—but his nerves were stinging by the time he circled the lot twice looking for shade. They even had greenery on the roof, it was one of those new eco-conscious buildings, but there was nothing even remotely resembling relief for metal chariots.

The nanny had a big floppy straw sunhat, and the kid had a green baseball cap. Neither of them reached for their own doors, so his job was even easier. Which should have pissed him off, but didn't.

Take that, Doctor Karsten. I'm just fine if I have something to do.

The library's refrigerated, vanilla-and-paper quiet enfolded them. The layout was yet another security nightmare, but at least he could keep the entrance—and the employee doors—in sight while he loomed at the edge of the kids' section, a giant scowling at a tiny foreign country. He stood, hands crossed and easy, watching as the kid twisted his baseball cap so the bill was in back and dragged her by the hand.

You'd think Marquez would buy his boy all the books he could read, but maybe the nanny just liked getting out of the house. Her hair, caught in a loose braid, glowed under UV-filtered skylights.

She could be any young mother, smiling fondly as Eddie careened from shelf to shelf, a constant source of gentle remonstrances and redirection. *We walk inside, Eddie. You can ask nicely, that means with a please.*

It was a shame she'd probably be gone before any of the training sank in. Still, Eddie obeyed each time, sneaking small glances at Vince. Did she usually play good-cop-bad-cop with Alan?

No, he decided, watching her yet again caution the kid to walk inside. She just played good cop all the time. Probably got taken advantage of by street hustlers, and probably never asked for a raise, either. In short, she looked like a real do-gooder girl, the type of oblivious that got cut down first when the shooting started.

That was a bad thought. His fingers tightened as a coltish, strawberry blonde preteen with a diffident grin full of silver braces and an armload of novels brushed past, blinking owlishly and entirely too close. Vincent was spending too much time staring at the nanny and not enough on the rest of the room.

To top it off, he'd forgotten her first name. Carol? Karen? Something like that.

The nanny glanced in his direction, an apologetic flicker of those large dark eyes. What did she expect, looking at him like that? He was an appliance, just like the car.

Eddie careened around the corner and almost into the preteen girl; Vincent braced himself for the collision.

"That's *enough*," the nanny said sharply, and every kid in the section stopped in their tracks. One or two adults did, too, glancing uneasily in her direction before slotting her into the young-mommy category and returning to their business. The kids took a little longer, palpably glad they weren't about to be scolded.

The boy stopped dead, hunching sheepishly. Halperin, that was the nanny's name. Miss Halperin. The first name still bobbed just outside his mental reach.

That wasn't normal either. He was distracted. *Too* distracted.

"Sorry, *señora*," Eddie muttered, all but digging his toe into the carpet. "Really."

"I'm not the one you ran into." Miss Halperin didn't raise her voice at all, but that tone could cut glass. She didn't fold her arms, but her posture was very straight. Maybe it was all the yoga. "I asked you to walk three separate times, Eddie. No storytime today."

Vince expected the kid to throw a fit. It was what any other spoiled brat would have done, especially one who knew his parent could fire the nanny at will.

But Eddie gulped, turned a few shades paler, and meekly regarded the girl with braces, his small arms just as loaded as hers. "I'm sorry I bumped into you," he said, formally.

"It's okay." The girl smiled kindly enough, metal in her mouth gleaming. She looked shyly at the nanny, and evidently took her big-kid social responsibilities seriously, breaking into a wider, very magnanimous grin. "It's okay. It's exciting to be here, isn't it?"

"Yeah." Eddie snuck a glance at the nanny, who nodded approvingly, her arms folded. "Sorry," he added in Miss Halperin's direction, and the look he turned on the nanny would make an iceberg melt. The kid knew he was cute, of course.

"Good job." Miss Halperin's smile held all the promise of complete forgiveness. "Let's go check those out, buddy."

His face fell, but Vince felt almost like cheering. It would do the kid good to get some consequences for his running around. It did *everyone* good to have a few rules, if only to know when to break them so you wouldn't get caught.

And the nanny didn't cave, just beckoned him away as a wide-hipped woman with a nametag, a flowered blouse, and a no-nonsense grey bun stalked into the children's section, greeted with a susurrus of excitement.

Eddie threw a mutinous look or two over his shoulder, but he obeyed. They checked the books out at a self-service station, then the nanny opened up the burlap bag and began carefully packing them by size. "This might take me a while," she said, softly, and glanced at Vincent. "Would you walk Eddie over to listen to the story while I get it done?"

I'm supposed to watch both of you. He swallowed the words, because she looked . . .what? Almost hopeful, and those big, quiet eyes seemed to stop his nerves from sparking.

Vincent nodded, sharply, and the kid managed to keep it to a slow jog, almost dancing in place for each of Vincent's strides.

And he *still* couldn't remember her first name.

SHE LET THE KID run at the park, though she packed him up well before he was ready. Or so Vincent thought, until they were in the car on the way back and he caught a glimpse of the little fellow nodding as he stared out the window. Eddie's chatterboxing had wound down, and they drove in something like companionable silence.

He had to admit Miss Halperin knew her stuff. It was an unexpected relief, and she was probably goddamn magic or something, because his hands had stopped ache-longing to curl into fists and the ringing in his ears had gone down. Or maybe it was just having a job, any job, to focus on.

By the time the Volvo had run enough for the air-conditioning to make a difference they were already back at the house, and there was no good reason for his remaining, persistent unease. Maybe it was just raw nerves, and the white sedan following them at a discreet distance was someone else who lived in the neighborhood. White cars were common, and he couldn't be sure it was the one he'd glimpsed before cutting the engine at the park *or* waiting to turn into the library parking lot. The shape was right, but they stayed just far enough away he couldn't see the license plate beyond noting it was in-state colors.

It could have been three separate cars, sure. Or one driven by a professional, one who knew how to stay just far enough back.

Even when they pulled into the garage, the nanny and the kid stayed put until he cleared the environment and opened the kid's door, though it was still too hot and they both probably longed for air-conditioned comfort. Still, the nanny in her blue dress didn't look wilted at all, though her forehead and the tender column of her throat glistened.

The kid banged his way inside. She lingered, loaded down with the burlap library bag, her purse, and another leather bag that looked far too big to be carrying around supplies for a six-year-old. Still, she managed them with the ease of long habit; Vince didn't even get the chance to offer help.

Not like she would have accepted, it looked like.

The house was still a chilly forced-air tomb, but Emilia had left for the day. Lean blond Tomas and redheaded Jakob, both much more relaxed with Alan gone, were doing grounds sweeps. Vince settled in the camera room with a scarcely audible sigh. There was a good ergonomic office chair back here, monitors blinking bleary-eyed in rows. The moving cameras threatened to give him motion sickness, but the worst was craning as if he could see something just out of the camera's range, his shoulders stiffening with immediate pain. He couldn't be a drone jockey; how those boys escaped migraines was beyond him. It would be nice, he supposed, to just sit in a trailer and press a button, all the blood and screaming grainy pixels on a screen.

Nice, sure, but hard on your damn neck.

Afternoon snack time meant both nanny and kid were in the kitchen, and Vincent watched her move between the fridge and the second island, the maxi-dress fluttering. It was almost indecent, the way the dress showed nothing but her shoulders while letting a man guess at everything else.

The kid's mouth moved; it looked like he was downloading at a high clip. There was no audio, and Vince wouldn't have turned it on if he had.

Or would he? Vincent realized he'd been staring at that particular monitor and ignoring the rest of his job. Empty rooms sat still or swung lazily back and forth, the externals showed a broiling late-summer afternoon. Tomas and Jakob had finished sweeps and were at the front steps discussing something or another; Vincent's nape tingled again.

It was the same feeling that warned him of ambushes, and he didn't like it. Most of all, he didn't like the idea that he was a mass of raw uselessness, scraping over innocuous things instead of seeing the real threats.

The gate-light blinked; it was the landscapers, well within their usual arrival time. The security on the front steps must have been waiting for them, because the redhead looked up at the camera and gave a thumbs-up.

Vincent toggled the gate. "Cara," he heard himself say, alone in a nerve center, a magician with invisible spider-strings all over the house. "That's her first name."

A pretty one, too. But to punish himself for inattention, he scanned every screen thoroughly.

Except the kitchen, where the kid applied himself to apple slices, peanut butter, and milk. Not to mention a certain black-haired woman's attention, the lucky little bastard. But Vincent didn't know that, because he didn't look.

At least, not very often.

Wrong Number

"ARE YOU SURE you won't stay for dinner?" Cara balanced a few round, nested Tupperware in one hand, peering around the fridge door. "Emilia left plenty."

"Thanks, but I got a date." Red-haired Jakob, his shoulders straining at a navy T-shirt, had an easy smile and managed to keep his gaze well above her neckline. His nervousness was faintly endearing, and certainly worlds better than Alan. If she didn't know better, she might even think Jake a little scared of a woman half his size.

"Congrats." She even tried to sound pleased, stacking containers on the pretty marble tile countertop. What did Em do if she dropped an egg? Good heavens. "Well, get out of here, then. Is Tomas staying?"

"Don't think so." Jake stuck his thumbs in his pockets, an entirely habitual pose. "You okay with the new guy?"

"He seems all right." She darted a glance at Eddie, who was too busy with a clutch of toy cars on top of the second kitchen island to pay much attention to boring grownup chatter. "I don't think he's made friends with the little guy, though."

"Kids, man. I'd rather face a mugger any day." Jakob lingered, one hand on the knob of the back kitchen entrance. Behind him, westering sunshine glared red and angry. It was the season of great sunsets, and in a little while the storms would sweep in. She was looking forward to the light shows. "You *sure* you're gonna be all right?"

"There's the security system, and the new guy. We'll be fine." But now, she wondered. The new guy was basically a stranger—but half the staff was still in that category as well, though Cara had been here for months. Fraternization was *not* encouraged under Marquez's reign, or Alan's for that matter. "Why? Is there something I should know?"

"Just makin' sure. I don't know why Señor put a brand-new dude on nights, or . . .well, never mind." Jake shook his head, a big healthy dog getting rid of an unpleasant thought. "See you around, Halperin."

"Thanks, Jake. Have a good evening." Any girl dating him would have to get used to the way he bit his fingernails, but that wasn't Cara's problem.

It was a relief to be able to stop caring about *something*.

Emilia not only tagged each container with masking tape, but also noted cooking time and temperature on anything Cara would have to heat up on days the queen of the kitchen was absent. It was a little thing, but it felt like a warm blanket. Em didn't *have* to do half of what she did, especially for a mere fellow employee.

"What's for dinner?" Eddie asked again as the back door closed. A breath of dust-freighted heat tiptoed into the kitchen's granite-and-steel gleam, falling spent as a dry autumn leaf when air-conditioning choked it.

"Looks like chicken provolone." *Although if it's not McNuggets, you probably won't like it.* The kid's palate was dismal, but then again, everyone under twenty-five had the same problem. Cara turned to the stove. "You know, you could go get Mr. Desmarais and ask if he'll have dinner with us."

"Don't wanna." Eddie's lower lip pushed out, sullenly. "Don't like him."

Cara suppressed a sigh. "Why not?" Her cell phone buzzed, rattling against the countertop, and she turned back to reach for it, almost knocking over the tower of glass, rubber, and plastic she would turn into dinner. *Whoops.* The disaster was averted just in time.

"I dunno." Eddie dropped a red car and scrambled off the stool to retrieve it. "I just don't."

Well, you can have your opinion, kid. I'll even be cautious until we see what this fellow's like. It was important to let children feel believed. Of course, it probably didn't help that the new guy was standoffish. Most of the security detail was. It had taken a long while for even Jakob to warm up to her. She shook her head, glancing at the phone.

It was Alan calling, and for a moment Cara contemplated picking up. An instinctive shiver of distaste went down her back. He could leave a message, she decided; if Mr. Marquez wanted to talk to her, he was welcome to call the house before Eddie went to bed.

The call went to voicemail. The man was a nuisance.

"Ma'am?"

Cara whirled, her heart in her throat and her elbow almost sweeping color-coded glass Tupperware off the counter.

It was Vincent Desmarais, in that same jacket, his chin set and his dark eyes unreadable. "You all right?" he continued, and Cara was just grateful she hadn't squeaked in surprise.

"You startled me." Her heart thundered in her ears, she had to work not to speak too loudly through the purely internal noise. "Speak of the devil, I was just about to send Eddie to get you."

"Ma'am?" His eyebrows rose faintly, a puzzled expression.

"Emilia leaves us something to reheat in the evenings when Mr. Marquez is gone; it's chicken provolone tonight. There's plenty for everyone, and we might even be able to sneak you a beer." *Since I know where Alan keeps his stash.* In her less charitable moments, Cara had played with the idea of distributing said stash among the security staff right before she dramatically resigned.

It was a satisfying fantasy, even if it would break her heart to leave Eddie, who clambered back up onto his stool and regarded Vincent with wide eyes, clutching the little red Hot Wheel in one hand.

He didn't like strangers. Marquez was always telling him not to trust people. *Everyone gonna try to do you, Eduardo.* It was a self-fulfilling prophecy for a truth that didn't need any help, as far as Cara was concerned. Six years old was too young to learn some things.

"Thanks, but no." Desmarais visibly caught himself. "I mean, no beer. Can't drink on the job."

"That's reasonable." Maybe he was just shy. She decided, tentatively and provisionally, that she liked him well enough. "Do you have any rules against chicken provolone on the job?"

For a moment his face closed down, shut like a heavy door in a windowless hallway. All the security staff affected military brusqueness, but she thought this guy might have actually served. Then, his mouth twitched at one corner. "Only if it's bad chicken."

Cara couldn't help but laugh. Eddie smiled uncertainly, his gaze darting between them. Her phone vibrated again.

Again, it was Alan.

Irritation zinged through her, like biting on tinfoil. She'd be a lot more inclined to answer his calls if they were ever about anything real. Oh, he'd find a reason to keep her on the phone—or at least, he'd try.

But he wasn't her employer, and he wasn't even truly her employer's proxy. So she hit the red circle that meant *ignore* with a knuckle-tip and fixed Vincent Desmarais with a steady look. "I don't think Emilia's capable of making bad chicken. There are plates in that cupboard, and the glasses are there. You're not lactose intolerant?"

"Not that I know of, ma'am." But the ghost of that smile lingered somewhere behind his mask, turning his dark eyes soft. It did good things for him. "I've been on KP before, I'll help."

"Good," Cara said, and opened the first container. "No help, no eat." It was one of Emilia's little jokes, and Eddie laughed, a high nervous giggle becoming natural halfway through and settling into one of the most infectious sounds, a child's chuckle.

HALFWAY THROUGH dinner the kitchen extension shrilled, and Cara slid off her stool quickly, lunging across the room to answer it on the third ring. "Marquez residence," she said, a bright crisp secretary's greeting. "Hello?"

The line wasn't quite dead; she could sense someone breathing on the other end. "Hello?" She tried again, turning to look at Eddie, whose forkful of chicken hovered in midair, his round little face full of dread. It was a little early to be his father, but you could never be sure.

The line clicked, then the dial tone filled her ear. Cara shrugged, setting the cordless back in its charger. "Wrong number, I guess."

"You sure?" It was a wonder the wooden stool—not the one Emilia used, but the one generally tucked under the counter at the narrow end—didn't buckle under Vincent's solidity. His back was to a wall instead of the door; it was probably why he'd chosen the spot. He hunched his shoulders when he addressed Eddie, visibly trying to make himself smaller, and Cara liked him even better for it.

"Guess so." She was halfway back to her place when the extension rang again. "Oh, for *God's* sake." She shouldn't be expressing any frustration in front of Eddie, but really, it had been a long day. Even in the air-conditioning, the heat wore on your nerves.

Desmarais slid off his stool and strode across the kitchen, bearing down on her. He passed very close; Cara, nailed in place, caught a whiff of leather, a hint of aftershave, the slightly acrid note of sweat on a healthy, otherwise clean male. He didn't shoulder her aside, but he did snatch the cordless up, jab the button, and growled, "Marquez residence."

She heard, and almost *felt,* whoever was on the other end slam the phone down. Desmarais replaced the cordless in its charger and glanced out the windows over the sink, then at the back door, both now bearing tired shadows in their corners as the light stretched.

Of course it was probably a redial by mistake; it happened all the time. There was no need to get into a tizzy, *or* to frighten Eddie. "It's not your dad, sweetie. He'd call the nursery extension."

Vincent turned back and gazed at her, his expression changing slightly as he studied her face. "Probably a wrong number, yeah." His agreement sounded grudging, but at least Eddie took it at face value.

The new guy even hovered anxiously as she settled back onto her stool, as if he wanted to hold her chair. A real gentleman.

Maybe he was. Still, Cara suddenly had no appetite, and she couldn't wait to get on her yoga mat and think about things.

Not out by the pool tonight, she decided. Maybe, just maybe she'd practice inside. For no real reason, except the heat.

Sure.

Like a Creep

THE MONITORS STARED at the camera room, unblinking eyes full of color-drained rooms. Vincent settled in the main chair and forced himself to check them all, especially the gate and the walls. There should have been a couple guys to share watch tonight, but maybe Klemp had told Alan that Vince was worth three or four guys all on his own.

It would be just like Paul, though Marquez seemed too careful to commit the mistake of leaving his kid practically alone in the house with a stranger. Cara was a real doll, as Vince's old squadmate Footy Lenz would have said, but she was no match for an armed man. For one thing, she barely reached Vince's shoulder, despite those long lithe legs.

For another, she was too trusting. She didn't watch angles, she didn't look out for anything but little Eddie; she was the very essence of an oblivious civilian. Which was *obviously* fine, her job didn't entail bodyguard duty and not everybody could be a professional, but still . . .it bothered him.

What bothered him even more was the persistent sense of being watched, and not by an employer's cameras. The fine hairs on his nape were tingling almost constantly, and wouldn't ol' Doc Karsten like to hear about that? It wasn't illegal to have side work when you were on leave—far from—but Karsten would probably hem and haw about how it wouldn't ameliorate fatigue or post-traumatic stress. He could almost *hear* the medic's prissy little objections.

The bigger worry, of course, was that Vince might be strung so tight he was seeing ghosts. Which meant he couldn't be cleared for duty.

And why, in God's name, would he feel unfriendly eyes on him *outside* the house? If he was jumping at shadows . . .

Finally, he let his gaze settle on the playroom screen. The nanny was in a low, wide wicker chair, the kid cuddled as close as he could get. Looked like she was reading to him.

Vincent winced. She was a nice, normal woman, and here he was watching her through the cameras like a creep. The kid fidgeted but she didn't seem to mind; each time he shifted, she made a subtle accommodating movement. That took real affection, impossible to fake because it was absolutely unconscious.

She probably brought home strays, gave her change to hobos, and would likely even stop to rescue a half-squashed animal in the road. A big old bona fide bleeding heart, with those huge dark eyes. What would it be like to sit that close to a real human being? That eternal figment of the imagination, a normal person; she'd probably get married to another unicorn, both of them baking cookies and going to PTA meetings.

He was a creep, and he had to stop staring. So Vincent searched the camera room, more to keep himself occupied than anything else.

Old security schedules were filed in a cabinet under the postage stamp of a desk, and the chicken-scratch writing was undoubtedly Alan's. Vincent's eyebrows drew together as he paged through the ones for the last few weeks, and he glanced across the monitors once or twice as he read, keeping an eye on everything.

All was as it should be there, but the schedule was odd. At first he thought it was only heavy while Marquez was home, which might just have meant his employer was a penny-pincher. What father wouldn't want his kid taken care of while he was away, though? There were all types in the world.

His wasn't to question why, Vince decided. At least not yet.

About a month ago, the handwriting on the schedules changed into vastly different chicken-scratches for about two weeks. Vincent studied it, and his nape wasn't just tingling. The cold flicking fingers slid down his entire back, and he felt a sliding sensation in his gut.

It wasn't that hard to read a roster. Hell, he'd written a few in his time. But this looked like the last time Marquez left on a trip, the security on the house wasn't reduced to bare bones. If anything, a few extra hands were hired.

He heard a faint, faraway shrilling; a blinking light on the desk phone was labeled KITCHEN. Vince hooked it up, pressed the button, and put it to his ear. He said nothing, holding his breath.

There was a short pause, the subliminal humming of a live line. Then, very deliberately, whoever was on the other end hung up.

Vincent glanced over the screens again. Cara kept reading; she probably hadn't even heard the phone. Blissfully unaware, with the kid just as close to her as he could get. Peas in a pod.

I should get out of here. The thought held the crystalline ring of truth and fear at once. Some jarheads, plenty of professionals, and even some high-speeds or fellow snake-eaters thought you lacked balls if you admitted being afraid. The real pros knew trepidation kept you sharp and alive, as long as you managed it and not the other way around.

There might be a reasonable explanation.

Yeah, and monkeys might fly out my ass, too. It'll happen any day now.

Vincent tensed, ready to spring out of the chair, gather his shit, and stop by the playroom to tell the nanny . . .

. . .what? What would he tell her? *I'm the new guy and you should come with me if you don't want to get hurt.* Or, even, *Run for the hills, doll, my neck feels weird and that means trouble.*

Yeah. That would fly *real* well. The kid would start to cry, she'd know he was a simple creep, and she'd probably call Marquez in hysterics. Klemp would kick his ass for ruining a good job because Vincent was a few fries short of a Happy Meal right now.

And he knew it.

There she sat, reading on a grainy screen, her lips moving softly and her expression changing in flickers with each word. She probably did different voices for every character, and he'd bet the kid loved it.

Some prank calls and a mistake or two on the security schedule—or, hell, even some employee-mice deciding on a night at play while the cat-boss was away—wasn't a good enough reason to scare the shit out of a really nice lady and a six-year-old. It might have been if Vincent was in top form, but he wasn't or he'd be on duty with his squad, doing real work instead of babysitting.

So he sat there like a creep, watching the screens, and trying to ignore the icy little spiderfeet running down his back.

It was probably nothing. Even if it wasn't, there wasn't anything he could do until the first flare popped.

Great.

It was little consolation that he felt like he was ready to ruck up again, and his nerves had settled.

HE DIDN'T SLEEP in the tiny monk's cell. For one thing, it wouldn't be prudent to stay where anyone could find him. For another, it was too far away from the nursery.

Instead, he carried a pillow to the playroom hall and settled near the door. It wasn't quite pleasant to be sleeping armed and in his boots again, but it was familiar.

Almost comforting.

It was also too quiet; the house was tightly sealed and even the whisper of cold forced air through curlicued brass vents couldn't penetrate the faint noise of blood soughing in his ears.

Even your own pulse could be an enemy.

It wasn't like sleeping rough. No matter how much care you took sweeping your space, there was always a pebble or a bump left. Even hammocks, beloved of forest fighters, were prone to stray jabbing branches and twisted coverings, not to mention the risk of being trapped when the flares popped, a tripwire snapped, or the subliminal metallic breath of a knife drawn from its sheath jolted a soldier into high-octane readiness.

One moment he was on his back, closing his eyes and breathing in the particular pattern you learned to keep oxygenated under fire. The next, he was in a crouch, the knife from under his thin pillow in his hand and his entire body a taut harpstring.

Cara let out a soft, surprised sound, probably only saved from being a yelp by the fact that the kid was asleep on the other side of the playroom. She dropped her rolled yoga mat and went sideways, her shoulder hitting the doorway; Vince's left hand shot out, closing around her ankle. He only meant to steady her, his fingers pressing hard, and she froze.

Vincent realized he was awake, crouching with a knife in one hand and his hand wrapped around the nanny's ankle. *Wait. How the hell did I get here?*

She inhaled sharply; he expected her to scream.

"Friendly," she said instead, soft but firm. "I'm a friend, Vince. Okay? *Friendly.*"

Did she think he was going to shoot her? Jesus. "Ah." He had to clear his throat, a harsh sound. Of course she could see well enough to recognize him; the playroom had one dim nightlight and the hall's recessed lighting was bright by comparison. "Oh. Yeah."

For some reason, his fingers didn't want to unclench. He forced them to and rose, hoping she wouldn't see the knife.

She'd changed into a tank top and loose linen capris; the lady set her bare foot down carefully, keeping her hands free and slightly away from her sides, a civilian's readiness. "Is there some reason you're sleeping here?"

"Um." He was ridiculously glad he'd brought a pillow and a blanket; Christ knew what she'd think if he was just lying fully dressed on the floor. "Yeah. Well, it seemed like a good idea at the time?" Vincent didn't mean to make it a question. His palm was burning with the feel of soft skin, so unlike his own.

Her mouth twitched. Vince watched, hypnotized, as she lost the battle and a smile dawned, tilting up the corners of her lips, crinkling the corners of her dark eyes, and just generally knocking the sense clean out of anyone lucky enough to witness the event. "I've had days like that. But really, is there a good reason why I shouldn't start screaming?"

Nobody's around to hear you, buttercup. "Figured my room was too far away if something happened."

It was almost physically painful to see that smile drain away. She stepped forward, her shoulders coming up, and he retreated. When she pulled the door to, bumping the rolled mat back inside the room, he realized she was protecting the kid, and a swift, sharp pain went through his chest.

It shouldn't have mattered. She didn't know him from Adam, of course she was being cautious. Still, a faint bitterness filled his mouth and he hurried to add details. "I mean, I'm the only one on deck tonight, ma'am. It didn't seem right to stay in my room."

"The only . . ." She absorbed this, a line appearing between her pretty eyebrows. She'd even look cute with a unibrow, for God's sake. It wasn't fair. "Wait. Bill and Marco aren't here? Or Tomas, he didn't come back?"

"No, ma'am." *Nobody here but us chickens,* he wanted to add, but it didn't look like she'd appreciate the joke. "It's just me. The schedule even says so."

"That's weird." She rubbed at her shoulder absently, those big eyes still fixed on him. "You're telling me there was no other security in the house last night?"

"No, Tomas and Bill were here after the party closed down." Was it morning already? He glanced at his watch—five a.m. "Just, nobody's here, not this past night. Maybe they decided since the big man's gone . . ." He trailed off, because she looked even *more* alarmed. So Vince stepped back and sideways, giving her space. Having a strange man loom over her first thing in the morning was probably unpleasant. His eyes were sandy, and that meant he'd been deep in slumber.

Maybe he'd been able to rest because he knew he was back on the front lines again. But that also brought up another question—what was *she* doing up at this hour?

"It's not like them." She moved as if to fold her arms, froze again. Those eyes were really extraordinary; they could yank a man clear off course with a blink or two. "Sometimes Mr. Marquez comes back without notice."

Mr. Marquez. Very formal, which was comforting. Or maybe she was just being careful to keep a relationship secret. Women liked money, didn't they? Rich men always had a flock of honeys.

And why should that thought make his hands ache again, and his teeth want to grind?

Vince had nothing to say, so he kept his mouth shut. She studied him, curiously. The silence stretched, almost uncomfortable.

"I suppose I'll go back to bed then," she finally said, cautiously. "You probably should too."

I should, huh? Sarcasm was the wrong note to strike, but for the life of him, he couldn't figure out the right one. "Yes ma'am."

He waited as she backed through the door, and heard the tiny click of a doorknob lock. It wouldn't do any good; he could put his shoulder down and break it in a trice. She was just being cautious, responsible with the kid's safety.

And probably heading for her cell phone to call her boss. Vince hadn't done anything wrong, but that was no guarantee for escaping trouble.

He thought about it for a long while, then gathered up his blanket and pillow. It was already morning, and if he stayed here she'd probably trip over him again when she gathered enough courage to come back out.

Vince didn't realize he was smiling at the thought.

Weekday Shoppers

CARA WENT THROUGH her morning yoga in the playroom instead of outside near the pool, hoping she wouldn't wake Eddie, and took her time cleaning up and dressing for the day. Finally, when she couldn't put it off any longer, she peered cautiously into the deserted hall before creeping out and down to the kitchen.

The coffeemaker stood silent sentinel, empty because it hadn't been programmed the night before and Emilia hadn't arrived at five-thirty sharp to press it into service. Cara didn't quite have goosebumps yet, but it was close.

Maybe everyone *had* decided to take a day or two off since Marquez wasn't going to be home, and she'd missed the memo. It wasn't as if she could join them—Emilia had an apartment in the city for the two or three nights a week she didn't stay in the small efficiency at the house, but Cara spent her nights right here, ready to leap into action when Eddie had bad dreams.

The big white house was silent as a tomb, and she winced. *Don't think those sorts of things. There's a good explanation.*

Now she had to worry about covering for the rest of them if Marquez called. Tattling on her coworkers wasn't an option, but on the other hand, what if something happened while the rest of the security staff was gone? And Vincent was a stranger, for God's sake.

All right. Make coffee, then figure out everything else.

She dropped a *Hey, what's happening* text to Emilia, another to Tomas, and set about making coffee and preparing for Eddie's breakfast. The cleaners were due today, and the pool guy as well.

One moment she was alone in the big, bright, antiseptically clean kitchen; the next, she turned and saw Vincent in the doorway to the employee hall.

At least she didn't flinch and yelp, but she did almost drop the container of half-n-half.

For a moment his dark eyes gleamed hungrily; his shoulders strained at a blue T-shirt and his short hair was damp, ruthlessly combed. He'd shaved, but he'd scruff up early; it looked like he'd won the stubble lottery two or three times over. And he carried, of all things, a clipboard.

He looked like some kind of inspector from the agency. But when he approached, oddly soundless in his heavy boots, and laid the clipboard on the tiled breakfast bar where she and Eddie always had dinner with Emilia, she saw it was the security schedule, with highlighting and crossing-out in both Alan and Tomas's handwriting.

"I'm sorry I scared you," he said, quietly. "Here."

Unless he was the world's greatest forger, it was there in black and white—or, more precisely, blue ballpoint and pink and yellow highlighter. Nobody was scheduled for the remainder of this week.

Or the entirety of *next* week.

She tried not to sigh and roll her eyes. It was just like Alan to keep this to himself. Maybe he thought she'd miss him or something.

Fat chance. "I wish someone would have told *me* about this."

Vincent's relief was palpable. "Yeah, well, me too."

"Why isn't your name on it?" She flipped a few pages back, then back further, just in case. If this was a practical joke or a prank, it was a good one.

"Probably because they're paying me cash." He stayed carefully on the other side of the island; this guy was probably used to his size making people cautious. "Gotta tell you, ma'am, I don't like this."

The kitchen tiles were chilly under her bare feet, and whatever calm she'd gained through morning practice was fading under a strange feeling hovering somewhere between irritation and uneasiness.

Cara's throat was dry, too. "I don't either," she said, finally. The coffeemaker began to burble, happily oblivious to the mounting unease. "I wouldn't blame you if you decided to bail, too."

"Yeah, well." His shrug was strangely graceful for such a big guy. Normally someone his size moved like a sack of concrete and walked heavy-footed as well. He was so *quiet.* "I wouldn't feel right, leaving you and the little guy alone."

It warmed her despite all reasonable caution, especially since Eddie was on a huge *I don't like anything new* kick. Kids his age had a hard time with any disruptions to their habits. Adults, Cara had to admit, weren't that different. "I think we'll be okay, if you've got to go." She pushed the clipboard towards him with her fingertips. He was glancing longingly at the coffee pot. "Milk? Sugar?"

"Huh?" He stared like she was speaking Swahili, or even French. "No, black. Thanks."

"Were you in the service?" They tended to frown on extraneous substances in their java, unless it was the distilled grain variety.

A short, clipped nod was all she received for her trouble, along with a curt, though polite, "Yes ma'am."

"But not anymore?" If she was going to be alone with him, it made sense to find out a little bit more.

His shoulders tensed, but only slightly. "Not at the moment."

Well, wasn't that an interesting answer. "Oh."

"Medical reasons, ma'am." He didn't move, braced on the other side of the island, probably aware he was on thin ice. "Not a dishonorable discharge, if that's what you're thinking."

"I'm not here to check your paperwork." Her phone buzzed; she finished pouring and scooped it up. *Huh.*

It was Emilia. *Didn't you know?*

Know what, Cara typed, and gave Vincent his coffee.

More texts followed. Apparently, Alan had told Em she was on paid leave for a couple weeks. Cara suppressed yet another deep sigh. It looked like she was going to have to cook for herself and Eddie—and probably this guy too—when the prepared Tupperware ran out.

As soon as Marquez got back, maybe she *would* turn in her notice or ask for another assignment. Dealing with Alan was a penance, but maybe she'd finally paid enough in that particular coin. There was a pinch under her breastbone the instant she decided as much, but she chalked it up to morning hunger and did her best to forget about the whole thing.

After all, they had a busy day planned, and she had to be home in time to let in the cleaners.

THE SALT SPRINGS Mall was a three-floor pile of concrete, glass, and overpriced food court; Eddie, of course, loved the place. Cara was neutral on malls in general, but she'd promised they could go looking for his daddy's birthday present. Eddie had been saving up change and his pittance of allowance, and she'd hinted to Marquez that while the little fellow was saving, a six-year-old might not have enough for a gift commensurate to his father's status.

Marquez had merely made a dismissive noise, but the next day Alan handed her an envelope containing three crisp fifty dollar bills, Eddie's name and *Cumpleaño de Papi* written on the outside in cramped, rounded letters. Of course Alan also smirked while he did so, but Cara just thanked him kindly and walked away, trying to ignore the sensation of her ass being stared at.

Vincent drifted behind them, threading through the weekday shoppers. It wasn't as crowded as it could have been, but every time she glanced over her shoulder as if he was a slightly older child she was responsible for, he looked exceedingly uncomfortable.

Who wouldn't be, in his situation?

Eddie kept a tight hold of her hand, especially when they stepped into the Model Emporium. Tiny replicas crowded each display case; to-scale planes, trains, vintage cars, even some architectural kits in brightly colored boxes sat self-satisfied in their appointed places.

"Which one?" Cara asked, but Eddie wouldn't choose until he'd seen everything the store had to offer, including the clear, stacked bins of parts in tiny plastic bags with cryptic symbols and strange notations on neat, even stickers. Vincent loomed behind them all through the store, a bull in a china shop carefully keeping his limbs away from every surface, visibly reluctant to even breathe heavily.

Eddie finally chose a replica of a low-slung yellow Viper, its box breathlessly listing its scale and amenities. It was clearly what he would most like to take home, divest of its packaging, and play with, and Cara hoped Marquez would understand that was the highest compliment a six-year-old boy could give. "Do you think he'll like it?" Eddie asked mournfully, and she hugged him.

"I think he'll be thrilled." She breathed in the salt-sweet scent of tumbled brown curls, and for a split second let herself pretend that he was hers. That she and Ben had finished painting the nursery, that she'd taken maternity leave and Ben kept working at Thomson Brothers Accounting where they'd met, and that this was a sneaky midday trip to get a proud father a birthday present.

Of course she shouldn't imagine, even a little. The agency had even warned against it, a patently ridiculous maneuver. Still, how could she *not*?

She could get her stuff out of storage, go back to an office job, maybe even get her yoga certification and teach a few classes. There was no reason to keep up the idea that had seemed so good at the time—responsible, even, dragging herself over a phobia in order to wear down its sharp edge like you were supposed to—but had turned into just another way of tormenting herself for something that hadn't even been her fault.

But part of being a grown-up was knowing when you were lying to yourself, and she wasn't ready to let go. She probably wouldn't ever be, and that was another part of adulthood—knowing you weren't going to take your own good advice, because you were too much of a masochist.

Fortunately, she was too busy to brood on *that* little realization. The acme of any mall visit, according to Eddie, was lunch in the food court and a whirl on the full-size carousel on the bottom level. There were rumors of an ice-skating rink in winter, but Cara hadn't been around long enough to see that yet.

It had still been a good summer, one she was grateful for. She might even make the supreme effort and submit the paperwork for another posting soon.

Just not this week.

Full of french fries and overprocessed meat, Eddie climbed onto a bright red wooden horse with a black mane, its neck frozen in a tortuous arch and its wide nostrils snorting highly carved and painted wooden fire. Cara settled sidesaddle on an ivory charger next to him, swinging her sunhat lazily and clinging to the pole.

Vincent apparently didn't hold with carousels. He watched from the other side of the barrier, and Eddie, excited enough to be forgiving, waved at him each go-round.

The big-shouldered man never waved back, just gave a tight, fractional nod each time. His gaze tracked them when they came into view, and each time they came around again, he found them and stared. Still, he seemed a little distracted, and the onlookers crowding the flimsy safety barrier unconsciously gave him plenty of space. He almost vibrated with tension, and Cara realized he barely ever smiled.

It was kind of comforting to have him along, regardless. Maybe when Marquez came back, she could put in a good word and the boss would hire the guy full-time.

Staying when everyone else bailed spoke well of a man.

Part of Valor

WHEN IT HIT, it hit fast.

Vince had marked one of them—a whipcord-lean fellow in a jacket very much like Vince's own who sat two tables away in the food court, pushing the contents of a chicken basket around and not eating much. The guy stood watching the carousel for a while too, occasionally looking at his cell phone. Vince actually told himself once or twice there was no reason to be alarmed—the guy was probably just a bystander enjoying Cara's pink and white dress and shapely, well-muscled calves, her wedge sandals and glorious dark mane added to that sinful mouth and large, liquid dark eyes.

Vince himself might have been distracted on duty by such a vision. But the tingling on his nape just wouldn't go away, and out in the parking lot under a flood of southwestern sunshine, all his subconscious muscles were tight and ready.

It was a textbook snatch, of course. They were even almost professional—a four-man team, more than enough to overpower a lone slab of muscle and grab two civilians. Or, to be absolutely honest, one and a half civilians, because if you took the nanny, the kid would follow.

What they didn't count on was the lone slab of stupid muscle being something *other* than a moonlighting cop or a weightlifter with a *Soldier of Fortune* fetish.

When the white van skidded to a halt, his hand was already closed bruising-hard on Cara's upper arm, shoving her almost over the kid. She went down hard, barking bare knees on pavement, and he couldn't afford the wince that went through him at the likely damage. She was now a much smaller target and covering Eddie, that was what mattered.

"Stay *down*," he barked, and the backman—the lean guy in the coat too heavy for late summer—hit him from behind. It would have been pretty effective, stunning if not putting him absolutely down for the count, if Vincent wasn't already moving. Maybe it was the whoosh of the telescoping baton cutting overheated air that warned him, maybe it was the fact that the van had been creeping along, maybe it was just his raw nerves twitching at the right time for once.

Vince's right shoulder exploded with pain, but he was more concerned about the guy rolling the van's side door open, combat boots hitting scorching pavement as he hopped out. Counting the van driver, there *had* to be a fourth, and he saw the "rattlesnake" coming from the other side of the nanny's Volvo, slices of reddening skin visible above the bandanna tied around his mouth and chin. Looked like he'd been waiting in the sun for a little while, probably ever since the guy behind Vince texted the targets' progress toward the exit.

Move, goddamn you, move!

It would have been easier with a gun, but he could almost hear old Sparky Lee Jones delivering his lecture on choosing the appropriate weapon for any scenario in a leisurely drawl.

When in a civilian situation, choose civilian methods. Or at least, methods that won't get you a weapons charge.

Sparky was an independent contractor, and he'd been teaching soldiers how to do hush-hush shit that never saw congressional inquiry for decades. He was a stocky bastard who never hurried unless he was beating the shit out of more than three guys at once, and he could track even the wariest creatures on God's green earth. For a pacifist—he'd never joined the service, though his sainted daddy had taught him all sorts of useful skills he made a living passing along—he was hellaciously good at mayhem. Still, he visibly hated what he was so gifted at teaching.

Vincent didn't mind so much. It meant that he was prepared when his squad was dropped into hostile country with a mission and he was doubly prepared *now*, when it counted.

The backman was raising his arm for another blow. Vince's left elbow caught him in the gut; he pulled forward and rammed the elbow back again, just managing to get the guy's face on its way down. Vince's right arm was a solid bar of agony, muscles seizing up as nerves telegraphed wild pain, but that was better than a skull-crack. The backman's baton clattered away between two cars, their tops and hoods shimmering with afternoon heat, and Vince pitched forward, hoping Cara would stay the fuck where he'd put her.

The rattlesnake with the bandanna—positioned to sweep Cara and Eddie into the arms of the heavyset guy just regaining his balance after jumping down from the van's open side—hesitated for a crucial fraction of a second. A real professional would have focused on his task, even if the backman was having trouble. These guys were probably used to snatching civvies, taking them just over the border, and storing them in oil drums while frantic families scrambled to come up with cash.

In short, they were real winners, and red rage bloomed just below Vincent's skin. The fury he'd gone into the service to tame—or at least harness—was an old friend, but thankfully it didn't blind him.

No, training turned it into a clinical, calculating fire, and it folded not only around him but also around the woman on the pavement, beginning to straighten in an instinctive reflex to avoid crushing the kid sheltered beneath her body.

No. Stay down. He stepped into the rattlesnake's strike range, his right arm obeying with an agonized, rusty drag of tissues protesting rough treatment and swelling to compress nerves. Still, he was faster than his size would let an onlooker guess, and his hand flashed out, smacking the baton from this man's hand, too. It clattered away and Vincent's foot flashed out; there was a greenstick *crack* as a knee was forced in a direction nature and physiology never intended.

The first real noise of the fight was a choked cry from the rattlesnake. The backman had gone down like a ton of bricks and was scrabbling on pavement for the van, reduced to a blind animal seeking shelter.

Vince considered putting two bullets in the driver's head just on principle, then dropping the snatcher just outside the van's side door. In-country, he would have *done* it instead of considering, but this was a civvie parking lot and the two packages had priority.

Cara had priority.

So it was a quick clip to the snatcher's ear to daze and confuse, then another snapping kick to a knee to put the third man down. He stepped at an angle again, between the snatcher and Cara. Backed up, hoping she'd get the message and move farther into cover with the kid. If the hostiles opened fire, Vince was a sitting duck, but his meat would stop the bullets from getting through. Someone was yelling a fair distance away—other civilians had noticed the fracas.

About damn time. Thank you.

The van's driver laid on the horn. Vincent, crowding Cara back, watched the snatcher drag himself into the van with adrenaline-laced speed. The backman and the rattlesnake, both deciding discretion was the better part of valor, hauled ass for that imperfect safety too; the vehicle was already in gear and rolling. The backman almost didn't make it, half-blind from instant swelling visible even through his bandanna.

They weren't used to prey fighting back.

Vincent took cover behind the Volvo, noting the van's license plate reflexively, his mouth full of copper adrenaline. Behind him, Eddie began to wail; his father's birthday gift was probably crushed. Cara was swearing in a soft undertone, but she was alive and presumably mostly unharmed.

Why he was considering that the most important thing, Vince didn't know. But just at that moment, before the first bystanders arrived and sirens began in the distance, it was enough.

THE INTERROGATION room was just like a debrief hole—one-way mirror, uncomfortable chairs, a flimsy table sticky with God only knew what, buzzing fluorescents, concrete floor easily hosed down. The only thing missing was restraints and maybe a car battery on a repurposed nightstand, ready to be pressed into service.

"We appreciate you chatting with us." The balding detective with the hard little pot belly—McIntyre—was the good cop, maybe because he was older. A man who liked his club sandwiches and beer a little too much might not be overly eager for blood. "You have no idea who these guys were?"

"Not a clue," Vincent agreed. He could have refused to say anything at all, but he wanted out of here. Hopefully Cara had enough sense to wait for him if they released her and the kid first.

In any case, Vince had the Volvo's keys. So right now, he could afford to play nice.

The younger detective—Sanderson, broad-shouldered and trim in the waist, dark-haired but with piercing hazel eyes—made a restless movement. *He* was the hungry one. "Oh, come *on*. You're working for Roderigo Marquez and you have no clue? I'm sure your military superiors will be real happy to hear about this."

Sanderson apparently enjoyed playing bad cop.

So Vince slowed down, using his squadmate Boom's shitkicker drawl for all it was worth. "I'm allowed to take a second job to supplement my income, sir." Boomer was a past master at evading shit duty and playing dumb with a deep, thick cornpone-and-gravy accent; Vince didn't mind being thought stupid if it got him out of here a little quicker. "Long as it don't interfere with my military duties."

"You're on leave?" McIntyre settled in his chair, looking at the manila folder he'd carried in. Oldest trick in the book, make an interrogation subject think you had him on paper.

Make him think you had *all* of him on paper. But Vincent really doubted even a quarter of the operations he'd pulled off would ever be committed to hardcopy a civilian police force could get its hands on.

"Medical leave, sir." He did his best to mimic Boom's *sah*, a single syllable that could hold respect, humor, and disdain—or all three, plus a leavening of anything else—at once.

"And working for cash, no doubt," Sanderson all but sneered, his arms high-folded. He was probably very aware he was pretty; maybe he'd been the good cop when they interrogated Cara.

For some reason known only to God or commanding officers, *that* thought was not guaranteed to keep Vince calm, so he shelved it. "That's between me and my employer." Vincent paused. "Sir." There was a way to let a pissant know you considered him just that, and you could tell a lot about a man by how he responded to it.

"Mr. Marquez is a very successful businessman." McIntyre shifted in his seat. Even though he was carrying at least thirty extra pounds—and that was a conservative estimate—his gaze was sharp-bright, and there was good muscle under the padding. He could probably tango for a whole round, maybe a round and a half before getting put down, age and experience giving him an edge. "There's no reason for him to be employing washed-up discharges when he could afford a whole lot more."

Vince let the insult slide. Maybe they were going to switch roles and the kid near the door would play good bozo for a while. Snapped back and forth, a weary perp would break sooner or later. It was inevitable, but Vince hadn't been reduced to name, rank, and serial number just yet.

Something was off here. He wanted some peace and quiet to suss it out, but until he got it, he'd settle for not fucking up his helpful-idiot routine.

"The plates you gave us were stolen." Sanderson didn't move, his arms folded and his light-eyed stare probably terrifying for a felon with a guilty conscience. The sociopaths would handle it just fine, though. "Looks like a planned kidnapping. You're a goddamn hero, Sergeant."

It's First Lieutenant, you prick. But okay. "Just doing my job, sir." He drew the *sah* out again, almost beginning to enjoy himself.

Almost. He'd feel a lot better if he had Cara and the kid in sight. Maybe the cops suspected as much, and were deliberately keeping him here.

"Why can't we get hold of Marquez to verify your employment?" McIntyre didn't stiffen, but his tone gave the whole game away.

"I have no idea, sir." Which was the absolute truth, and the staticky, creeping sense of incipient ambush returned. *Been here long enough. Get your packages and get moving.* It was time to move. "Am I being charged with something?"

"No," Sanderson had to admit. McIntyre didn't quite hurry to his feet, but it was close, his chair's feet making an agonized sound on aged linoleum.

"Then I'd better get Ms. Halperin and young Mr. Eduardo home." Vince unfolded, nice and slow, but he didn't miss the way both cops tensed. He didn't quite drop the drawl, but he did let some of it slide. "Unless you're charging *them* with something."

"They're being treated for—" Sanderson subsided when McIntyre glanced at him. The older cop dug in his suit jacket, coming up with a creased, battered handful of business cards.

"Marquez is a slick customer," McIntyre said, tweezing one semi-cardboard rectangle out of the pile. "If you see something that doesn't feel right . . ."

How long have you been after him? It was useless to ask, so Vince just nodded and took the card. He didn't promise—hell, he didn't say anything at all—but McIntyre's expression changed as if he had, and Vince pushed past young, eager Sanderson with barely a glance. He wanted to see Cara.

The world had become very simple, and Vince couldn't say he minded.

Good Behavior

VINCENT SAID LITTLE on the way home, driving the black Volvo with punctilious care as if he suspected the cops were following. Cara took the middle seat in the back so she could keep her arm around Eddie in his booster. Eddie wiped at his cheeks, clutching the crinkling paper bag with the model Viper; thankfully, the box had skittered under the car instead of being crushed.

Her palms were scraped, and her knees too. They both stung, doused with antiseptic and hurriedly but professionally bandaged. The ambulance workers had been the only soothing part of the whole thing; she'd ended up sitting on a hard plastic chair with Eddie in an "interview room", flinching each time a door slammed or a phone rang. Her skirt was dirty, her hair was awry even though she'd managed to yank it into a clumsy ponytail, and Eddie kept stealing sneaking little glances at her. If she lost her cool the kid would crack, and somehow, knowing as much made it easier to keep her face a tranquil mask.

They'd kept Vincent far longer than they questioned Cara. Eddie, big-eyed and clinging, hadn't been taken away to be interrogated separately; she was grateful for that, at least.

How long have you been employed by Mr. Marquez? She wasn't employed by him, she was contracted out by the agency, here was the paperwork. *Where is Mr. Marquez?* She didn't know, he often went on business trips and short vacations; that was why plenty of rich people had nannies. *What happened to the kid's real mother?* She didn't know, it wasn't her place to ask—that was her answer, at least, though Marquez had told her the bare bones, a car accident and a dead wife.

Eddie had shuddered, curled up in her lap, and at that moment, Cara decided it was time to go on the offensive herself, so to speak. The agency retained legal representation for certain occasions, she could call them—but no, the cops didn't want that. *Did you recognize any of the men?* How could she? It had happened so fast, and the only one she'd gotten a good look at had a bandanna over his face. He'd had brown eyes, she thought, but she couldn't be sure. *Had anything like this happened before?*

Not to her, and if they wanted to know more, she needed a lawyer present; in any case, she had a very upset little boy to get home.

Thank God she kept the requisite sheaf of official paperwork proving she had the right to schlep Eddie around, signed by the agency contact and Marquez, in her purse.

Why can't we reach Mr. Marquez? How in the holy hell should *she* know? She had them dial her cell phone and listen, getting nothing but Marquez's voicemail again. She even tried dialing Alan, for God's sake, but he didn't pick up either. *Did they often go without answering?* No, never before, and she wanted a lawyer present before they asked her another goddamn question.

That put an end to it, and sitting in a plastic chair in a busy police station hallway with a kid on her lap was a new experience. She'd tried to act like everything was normal for Eddie's sake, but her sigh of relief when Vincent showed up and said *Let's go* probably put the lie to any acting ability she ever possessed.

"Were they bad guys?" Eddie asked, his small, piping voice sounding very forlorn. "They looked like bad guys."

How in God's name was she supposed to answer? She didn't have to, because Vincent did.

"Maybe," he said, easily. His gaze was on the road and his big, hard-knuckled hands on the wheel at ten and two o'clock just like they taught you in driving school. "They certainly didn't seem very nice. How's your car, Señor Eduardo?"

It was just the right tone for soothing a kid—calm patent truth, not shaky at all. Maybe they taught people that in the military.

"It's fine." The boy peered into the crackling paper bag. "It went under the big car. I was afraid it'd get crushed."

"Well, it didn't." Vincent's gaze flicked to the rearview; he turned past the *Silver Heights* sign. Familiar landmarks began to slip by—the park undulated lazily on their left, which meant they were almost home. "Everything turned out okay."

Of course someone should reassure the little guy; Cara should have done it herself. Eddie gave her another nervous sidelong glance.

"That's right." She aimed for a normal tone as well, or at least, a calm one. She suspected she was still shaking, and every once in a while her shoulders would jump almost to her ears as if she expected a punch. "It was scary, but it's over now."

"Where's Pa—I mean, Dad?" It was a reasonable question; a boy would want his father after today. A distant, domineering patriarch might even be a comfort, a god capable of righting a tilted planet.

I wish I knew. Cara wasn't even a replacement parent, just an employee. Sometimes Marquez mentioned where he'd be going; most times he didn't bother, letting Alan give her the good news. And Alan hadn't this time. "He's probably on an airplane. If he is, he'll get my messages when he lands." Her head throbbed. So did her knees, her palms, her heart. Her neck wasn't far behind. It had happened so *fast.* One second she was just walking along, the next she was on hands and knees over Eddie as if they were roughhousing in the playroom, except with copper filling her mouth and everything inside her shrieking-loose with fear.

"He didn't say he was going on an airplane." Eddie gazed mournfully out the window. "He's gonna be mad."

Maybe. "Not at us. We didn't do anything wrong; those men did." *Get him off the subject, Cara.* She took a deep breath, wishing she was steadier. Braver. "We'll have a snack when we get home. Do you want pretzels or apples with your peanut butter?" Kids functioned better when you gave them two options, max; too many choices and they vapor-locked.

Cara was thinking adults were the same way.

"Pretzels." It wasn't even a contest, Eddie loved the crunchy stuff. "If Papi gets mad, he might send you away."

"We'll see." *He might not get a chance to. The agency's not going to be happy about this.* In any case, Eddie didn't need to think about *that.* It was, in childcare speak, a Big People Problem, and a strict division was kept between those and Problems Little People Sometimes Had.

"I don't want him to send you away." Eddie's lower lip pooched out and his eyes glimmered.

"He won't." Vincent braked and turned left; he was taking a roundabout route to the house. Cara's heart thumped as she realized as much. "It's not her fault, he won't send her anywhere."

Cara winced internally. *You shouldn't lie to a kid, sir.* But what choice was there?

"He sent Mami away. Alan told me." Eddie hugged the crinkling paper bag even harder.

That's enough. "Alan says a lot of things," she hedged. At least the EMTs had bandaged her up, but she was going to be stiff tomorrow. "When we get home we'll make sure the model isn't banged up, and we'll wrap it. That'll be fun."

Eddie didn't look at her. Vincent said nothing else, just made another few turns, circling the house like a shark.

THE VAST HOUSE was eerily quiet. Nobody had returned, and if the pool man or the cleaners had come by, she couldn't tell. Nobody was around to let them in, so it was academic.

It was also too late for snack—the cops had kept them for hours—but she made it anyway, and left Eddie perched on a stool at the breakfast bar with Vincent looming near the stove. "Hang on a second, buddy. I've got to get something, I'll be right back."

Thank God Emilia had told her where the key to the big glassed-in liquor cabinet was. Most of the bottles were purely decorative and probably full of cheap tea, but there was some good bourbon hidden on the third shelf.

Even if Marquez decided to fire her over it, she needed a shot of something to get her through *this*.

Vincent didn't even raise an eyebrow when she returned with the bottle. He'd refused treatment from the EMTs, though a glaring bruise was crawling up the back of his neck. His shoulder must have hurt, but he didn't *move* like it did. Maybe it was the adrenaline still soaking into all that muscle.

It was disturbing, how quickly the world could veer off course and disintegrate.

"You want some coffee?" Her hands shook, but she managed to pour a healthy slug of bourbon into a cut-glass tumbler. Eddie watched, wide-eyed and munching on pretzels.

"No ma'am." Vincent took a step towards her, cautiously, hunching a little. Whether it was because the adrenaline was wearing off or he wanted to look smaller and less threatening, was beside the point. "I'll take some of that, though."

So beer on duty wasn't okay, but this was? Or maybe the situation called for it; God knew *she* thought it did. "I thought you'd want it *in* the coffee." She snagged another tumbler and poured him a healthy dollop. "I . . .thank you, Mr. Desmarais. I don't know what . . . I mean, thank you." Two pale little words, unable to convey anything close to the depths of her gratitude.

"You're welcome." He took the glass with surprising delicacy and knocked its cargo far back, not quite grimacing afterward.

Now she knew how fast he could move; and Cara had been all but useless, huddling over Eddie. She should have done something, *anything*, to protect the little guy.

"You did great, by the way."

Had he read her mind? "Not really." Maybe her expression was just that transparent. She had to suppress a guilty start, capping the bourbon bottle. One jolt was fine, but there was Eddie, watching them solemnly. If she didn't model good behavior, who would? "I just sat there." *Like a bump on a log.*

"You stayed where I put you and protected Eddie." Vince glanced over his shoulder, making sure the boy was still perched where he should be. Was it good for a kid to hear this? "That was all you had to do."

Oh, was that it? She longed to ask him about the cops, about Marquez, about who those guys in the parking lot were—but Eddie didn't need that mental fuel. If he didn't have nightmares tonight it would be a blessing.

Hell, it would be a miracle if *she* didn't. "Well, they told us at the agency that stuff like this happens." Her stomach turned over, bourbon fighting for release instead of bolstering her. If she was calm, Eddie would be too. Right? "Money makes people do strange things."

"Yeah." Whatever Vincent would have added was lost in a high shrilling, and Cara jumped, letting out a soft, alarmed cry.

Eddie squeaked too, and before she was aware of moving she was next to him, her arm around him as he teetered on the stool.

"It's just the phone, it's all right." Her heart hammered in her ears, and all her scrapes and bruises throbbed afresh. "I'm sorry, sweetie. It's just the phone, it startled me too. It's okay."

Vincent half-turned, looking at the kitchen extension. It shrilled again and his eyes darkened, his mouth turning into a thin hard line. Seen in almost-profile, he was startlingly handsome, a wild creature breaking camouflage for a moment to test the wind.

"Don't you wanna answer it?" Eddie stared at him too. The boy's eyes were round as dinner plates.

"Not right now," Vincent said, the last word swallowed by yet another ring.

The boy, a pretzel halfway to his mouth, glanced at Cara before asking, "Why not?"

"The phone's a convenience, kid. Not an obligation." Vincent actually seemed to swell, drawing himself up between them and the landline as if he expected it to leap off the wall and attack.

The ringing stopped, and Cara let out a high-pitched, jagged little laugh. Eddie had gone pale.

Pull yourself together, for God's sake. Something awful is happening here, and he's just a little kid. "It's all right—"

Then her purse vibrated, her cell phone tinkling, and she almost clapped a hand over her mouth to trap another small scream.

"Don't answer," Vincent said, but she was already digging. The screen said *Dracula Cowboy*, and she swallowed a hot flare of anger, thumbing the green button.

"Hello?" *So help me God, I'm going to get some answers.*

"Hey, *chica*." Alan was outside somewhere, wind and traffic almost enough to obscure the words. "Miss me?"

Don't even start with me, Alan. "How can I miss you if you're calling me?" She drew in a short sharp breath, ready to launch into a barrage of questions.

"Aw, don't be like that." At least *he* sounded normal. All this would probably be just in a normal day's work for him. "You okay? You sound strange. Where are you?"

I was almost kidnapped. Or maybe they'd only wanted Eddie. Cara forced herself to breathe, daily practice coming in good stead. "I'm fine." *No thanks to you.* "Listen, Alan, something's—"

"That's good." He wasn't really listening, though. "Listen, I got some bad news."

Oh, more? That's great. "Bad news?" she repeated, stupidly, and found herself staring at Vincent.

"Yeah. Señor's been arrested at the border."

Cara almost swayed. Her gaze stuttered to Eddie, who craned his neck to study her. He was so small, and suddenly she was on her hands and knees again, scorching pavement stinging skin, knowing her body was the only shield between him and whatever madness was tearing the parking lot apart. "At the border?" *I sound like I've been punched.* All her questions fell away, spiraling into a black hole of shock.

"Yeah. Listen, I can't talk much." Sound of movement, cloth sliding. "Where are you?"

"At home," she said, stupidly. "Of course. Where else would we be? Alan, something's happened. We went to the mall and—"

"Good, good." Still not listening, of course. Just like a man. "We'll take care of this and señor will be home soon too. How's the kid?"

What do you mean, we'll take care of this? You're not a lawyer. "Fine," she heard herself say. A glass jar had descended over her, trapping her like a butterfly—just bumbling along, minding its own business, then netted and forced into a transparent prison. "He's just fine. Alan, you have to *listen* to me—"

The phone went dead, and she stupidly repeated "Hello?" a couple times before holding it at arm's length as if it was a venomous, wriggling thing. Had he been cut off?

Or had he just hung up?

"Who was that?" Eddie asked, and even his lips were pale. He clutched a pretzel in one small hand.

Be calm, Cara. Be very calm right now. "That was Alan," she said, and set her phone down, very carefully. The bourbon burned in her stomach, a comforting warmth, and she met Vincent's dark gaze. The unspoken message—*not in front of the kid, for God's sake*—flashed between them on invisible telegraph wires, and Cara set her shoulders. "He couldn't talk long. Finish up your snack."

Disturbing

EMILIA HADN'T LEFT any more of those meal-prep Tupperwares, but Cara was a handy cook. She could even flip an omelette, a skill Vince had never been able to acquire. She *also* stood up well under the pressure, calmer than a lot of civilians after a snatch attempt. She settled on the floor of the playroom with Eddie and a roll of wrapping paper after dinner, patiently teaching him how to fold and tape as if nothing in the world was wrong. The result looked pretty professional, except for the kid's loop-scrawled, handmade card.

Looked like Eduardo loved his dad. Well, Vince had loved his too, the violent asshole. It was as natural as sunrise, and as deadly as friendly fire.

Cara's brittle cheerfulness lasted all through the routine of getting the kid fed and into bed, and little Eddie took his cues from her. If he truly understood what had almost happened in the parking lot, he gave no sign. It would have been nice to be six and oblivious again, Vincent thought, especially since the kid could throw his arms around Cara and put his face in her throat, breathing her in.

They warned you about high emotion causing attachment when you were looking after a package, and there were strategies to minimize that risk. Once it happened, your effectiveness went down in some areas.

But Vince found himself thinking it probably went *up* in others.

Sparky might've agreed. It would have been nice to hear his old teacher's voice again, and that was a sure sign Vince's head wasn't clear enough to handle whatever was going on.

Finally, Cara closed the playroom door and stepped into the hall, rubbing at her temple with delicate fingertips. "He's down," she said softly, as if fearing her voice would float into the kid's bedroom. A long-sleeved thermal shirt clung to her upper half, and she was back in her loose workout pants. Maybe she wanted the arm-covering because of the air-conditioning, or maybe bruises were rising and she didn't want the kid to see. "I think he's okay. A little afraid, but . . .what are we going to do?"

So it was *we.* That was good. Vince had been sitting on a nasty supposition for hours now, waiting to broach it with her.

Now he found he couldn't, because she gazed up at him, worried and trusting, those big dark eyes open and vulnerable. *What are we going to do?*

"We're probably safe enough here," he said heavily, aware it was half a lie. Still, this place was familiar. He knew the ground and the blind spots, there was an alarm system, and he could hold the playroom door for a considerable length of time. The bars on plenty of the windows were nice and thick, too, which would help to funnel attackers. It wasn't perfect, but it was better than nothing. "For a couple days at least. What *exactly* did Alan say?" Now that the kid was down, getting the full sitrep would do them both good.

He should have coaxed the full story from her earlier, but both she and the kid were brittle. Besides, like the old song said, you didn't need a goddamn weatherman to tell which way the wind blew.

Now he was thinking of Sparky again; the old man liked his classic rock.

"He said Marquez was arrested at the border." Cara shivered, hugging herself. "That he couldn't talk, and he'd call back."

It was wrong. Everything about this was. Vince's gut couldn't get any more uneasy, so his back and neck got in on the action, running with prickles. There wasn't anything to do at the moment, so he ignored them. "Did he say by who?"

"No." A faint line appeared between her eyebrows. She lifted her arms slightly as if to hug herself, dropped them again. Even her pretty fingers were trembling. "Does it matter?"

If we want him back alive, yeah. "Not sure," he hedged. Right now he had all the problems he could handle—or more precisely, all the problems he *wanted* to handle. "What else?"

"I think he was distracted." She glanced nervously down the hall. There was no sound except the air-conditioning.

"You told him we're here, right? At the house?" When she nodded, Vincent squashed the faint vibrating panic behind his breastbone. Getting the squirrels wouldn't help anything, goddammit. "Did he ask?"

"Not specifically; he just asked where we were." She bit her lip, teeth sinking into softness, and that was powerfully distracting. Was she going to stretch tonight? Her palms were scratched up from the pavement, but she was moving all right. She wouldn't really stiffen up until tomorrow; Vince wasn't looking forward to his shoulder's future protests if he managed more than a light doze tonight. "I don't think he really cared. He sounded busy."

Didn't even give her a chance to get her own news out. Vince didn't like that, either. "Does he usually listen to you?"

"Are you kidding?" Even stunned disbelief looked good on her. "Alan's only interested in one thing."

"What's that?" *It better not be what I think it is.* And how strange was it that Vince was all of a sudden feeling possessive over a woman he barely knew?

"Himself." She folded her arms, this time overriding a wince and digging her fingers in, and there it was again—that fragile, heartbreaking determination, courage much deeper than Vince's own.

After all, he was trained for this shit and he had several inches on her, not to mention pounds of muscle. All she had was sheer bravery. And maybe some affection for little Eddie. "He sounds like a real winner."

"You have *no* idea." She probably had no idea she was hugging herself; no wonder she hadn't immediately dialed Alan back.

Vince's arms tingled. It would have been nice to get her close, reassure her a bit. But she might think he was just like Alan.

Was he? At the moment, he couldn't tell. "Is it usual for everyone else to vanish when Marquez goes on a trip?" He'd asked before, but he wanted to be absolutely sure.

It would help him plan.

"Of course not. He comes back with no notice sometimes. But this time he gave them a couple weeks off with pay and didn't tell me." A curious look stole over her face, and Vincent waited. Civilians needed time to think; he just needed a few seconds to react. The difference wasn't entirely training.

But the training helped. "He did?" he finally prompted.

"Emilia said Alan told her and Tomas about it. It isn't like Mr. Marquez to pay them if they're not working, but . . .I guess it's possible. He would certainly leave it in Alan's hands; maybe Dracula Cowboy's making himself popular."

"Dracula Cowboy?" Vince's mouth twitched. He couldn't help it. The name was incredibly appropriate.

She rolled her eyes, like a teenage cheerleader. "*Don't* tell him I said that."

"He won't hear it from me." No, not a cheerleader, he decided. She'd be an artsy type, one of those quiet girls everyone liked but nobody thought they had a shot at. The kind you knew would leave a small town in their rearview mirror and make it in the city, the type Vince barely looked at because it was useless to even dream. "Listen, ma'am—"

"It's Cara. I think we're past the ma'am bit, don't you?" Now she was even more anxious, rubbing gently at her upper arms. Shock wasn't a danger at this point, but he should still keep a watch for it. "I mean, you saved my life."

Maybe. They could have been just interested in the kid. "Just doing my job." It wouldn't do any good to let her think otherwise, or to let her in on his suspicions. Especially about Alan de la Cruz. "Anyway, do you have a place to go if this gets bad?"

It was already bad. Getting her out of the fallout was a good move—if she'd go for it.

"I've got my passport, if that's what you mean. But Eddie . . ." She shook her head a little too hard, driving away a bad thought. "His mom's dead. Car accident, I think. If his dad's arrested, where does that leave him? A foster home, CPS?"

Car accident? Alan told the kid his dad sent her away. Vince didn't feel like telling Cara what *that* might mean. It could just be a kid's misunderstanding.

The trouble was, there were too many coincidences and misunderstandings piling up. He didn't like this at all. Then there was the fact that his nerves were hamburger and the doctors were using nice little terms like *combat fatigue* and *paranoia.* And that grandaddy of diagnoses, *post-traumatic stress*, which was a long-term ticket to nonfunctioning.

He couldn't afford to be nonfunctional. Right now, Vincent Desmarais needed to be tiptop.

"This is a nightmare," she said, softly.

He swallowed, hard. This brave, fragile woman didn't have any idea what *nightmare* really meant. And he knew, all the way down to his bones, that he never wanted her to find out.

Which meant he had to do some thinking. But first things first. "Well, we're in it together, whatever it is."

Cara surprised him again. "Why?" Her expression wasn't exactly mistrustful, but it was cautious.

The caution cheered him up, even as it made a strange sharp pain go through his chest. "Why what?"

"I'm really grateful, don't get me wrong." She probably used that placating tone a lot on de la Cruz. "But I'd like to know why a virtual stranger's sticking around for this."

Smart lady. "It wouldn't be right to leave you and the kid in the lurch, ma'—I mean, Cara."

She studied him for what felt like a decade or two, thoughts moving in her deep, dark eyes. "So you're an honorable soldier."

Hell no, ma'am. I'm the bastard on the ground who gets the job done. But . . . "I'd like to be." That was the truth, or *a* truth, at least as far as she was concerned. "I'm trained for this, I took the job, and I'm going to see it through. Okay?"

She didn't answer immediately, simply studied him afresh. He'd been under some searchlights in his life, but never with a pair of soft, liquid dark eyes digging right through every defense and touching something he hadn't even known existed deep-buried inside his own head.

And, to be absolutely honest, inside his high left ribs too, as well as *significantly* lower down. She could give even the most hardened interrogators a run for their money.

Whatever she saw must have satisfied her, because her slim shoulders sagged and she leaned against the playroom door. "All right," she said quietly. "Good enough."

And Vince found himself hoping, from his haircut to his toes, that he would prove to be.

SHE RETREATED TO do her nightly yoga, and Vince used the time to go through the house top to bottom—except the playroom, of course—and get the cameras situated. There were a thousand and one blind spots, certainly, but he could train the electric eyes on the most likely routes for anyone who wanted to get their hands on the kid.

It was small comfort that he knew how *he'd* do it, so he knew how to arrange the defenses. He couldn't be sure if the next attempt would be semi-professionals like the snatch team in the mall parking lot, or *actual* professionals, with the gear to match.

Hell, he couldn't even tell if there would be a "next attempt." It troubled him that the cops had merely questioned and turned them loose. It also troubled him that they hadn't sent Cara and Eddie to the hospital, and hadn't wanted to impound and process the Volvo for evidence of the rattlesnake. Then again, they couldn't be sure any of the would-be kidnappers had touched the car, and they seemed to think the entire thing was just a scuffle, possibly not even a snatch attempt at all.

What did they know that he didn't? If Marquez was on the wrong side of the law, they could just be waiting to see. But it wasn't like cops to leave a six-year-old in the line of fire.

Was it? Vincent didn't think the young Detective Sanderson would look kindly on that shit, but you never could tell about anyone with a badge. It wasn't like the service, where you knew exactly what you were dealing with at any stripe level—mostly shit, but shit with rules. It was the considered opinion of Vincent's buddies that if the cops were any good, they'd be in a branch of the goddamn service themselves. The badge was for those who couldn't handle boot camp—or who had washed out.

He tried to keep his mind occupied with figuring out whether or not calling some of the squad was a good idea. It was both preparation and penance to take his time with setting up the house. He could have hurried back to the camera room and watched her bending and stretching, lithe and supple, her hair pulled back and her eyes closed, her breathing coming in deep even swells. The thought caused a few interesting reactions, especially below the belt.

He was pretty sure he could watch her all *day*, but how sick did that make him? It wasn't battle stress. He was downright broken, and he knew it.

She wasn't.

The hippies had it right, Sparky had said once after about six beers and a fuzzy number of tequila shots. *One two three, what are you fighting for? Once you decide that, all the rest of the killing's easy.*

He was right, as usual. It hadn't taken long for Vince to find out *how* right.

It was *disturbingly* easy.

Fortress, Prison

CARA SPENT THE night on the floor next to Eddie's bed. She just couldn't make herself stay in her own, and when she surfaced, blinking, to her cell phone alarm vibrating under her pillow, Eddie had slithered out of the red race car and curled up beside her, his thumb in his mouth and his olive cheeks rosy with slumber.

Dawn was rising; the house brimmed with sepulchral hush. Eddie didn't wake when she put him back in his bed; Cara straightened, rubbing at her lower back. Pretty soon he'd be too big to carry. By that point Cara might be in another job, and he'd barely remember a woman who had fed him, bathed him, crouched instinctively over him in a hot parking lot while the world went mad.

There had been no night terrors, but maybe that was only because he'd been too worn out.

Or because his father was gone. They both slept better with Daddy Dearest away.

Señor's been arrested at the border.

Now, with the benefit of a good night's sleep, she winced at how stupidly she'd handled all of this. She had to call the agency—but what on earth could they do? Would Eddie end up in foster care? It was an unappetizing prospect, to say the least. It was entirely possible Marquez would bail himself out and come home, and if he found his kid taken into state custody he was apt to get unpleasant.

Something else bothered her, too. Normally Alan wouldn't get off the phone until she hung up on him. But yesterday he'd been in a hurry, wouldn't listen to a damn thing she said, and wanted to know precisely where she was.

I don't want to be thinking what I'm thinking. Cara smoothed the sheet and blanket over Eddie and padded softly away. She stopped in the middle of the playroom to do a few sun salutations, wincing as her body reminded her of yesterday's jolts. All in all, though, the stiffness wasn't as bad as she'd feared.

The hall outside the playroom door was deserted. The kitchen, however, was full of bright warm light, and the coffeemaker burbled pleasantly. Vincent was at the sink washing his hands, broad shoulders straining at a navy T-shirt. Either it was yesterday's or he had more than one; she couldn't imagine he'd taken the time to do laundry.

So he hadn't left. Painful tension she hadn't even been aware of fled Cara's own shoulders. "Good morning."

He shrugged and grabbed one of Emilia's much-bleached flour-sack towels. "Coffee's on." A husky start-the-day growl, gravel in his throat even though he didn't smoke.

"You're a true gentleman." She headed for blessed caffeine. She should do a proper practice, but lugging her mat out to the poolside didn't seem . . .

Well, it didn't seem quite *safe.*

"Never been accused of that." He finished drying his hands, half-turned so he could rest a hip against the counter, and examined her from top to toe. The second island was clotted and crowded with papers, and Cara's stomach turned over. "I went digging. You're not going to like this."

"Because there's so much about this situation to love already." Cara glanced nervously at the kitchen extension, but the phone just sat there, black and cordless, a silent witness. She was in her pajamas, for God's sake, and ludicrously unprepared for the direction this conversation, let alone the entire world, was heading. "I take it you went through Mr. Marquez's desk."

"File cabinets too." At least he didn't sugarcoat it. "Especially the locked ones. You must have suspected he's not quite on the side of the angels."

Cara focused on pouring coffee. At least it stopped brewing when you took the carafe out. "He passed the agency background check." It was a prim, unhelpful thing to say, and it made her sound complicit.

Everything did, she supposed.

"And by the time you figured out he wasn't completely kosher, you were already in love with the kid." He folded the towel up with prissy exactitude, setting it back on the counter instead of hanging it up. "It happens."

Cara opened her mouth, but her cell phone vibrated on the counter. This time it wasn't the alarm, just a call. Coffee slopped inside her white china mug, and she almost let out a tiny, wounded little cry.

"That's probably Alan," Vincent said. His eyes were very dark, and his mouth was a straight line. "Tell me I'm wrong."

Cara picked up her phone. Her heart triphammered, and her hand shook. But she punched the green button anyway, and lifted it to her ear. "Alan." She tried to sound severe instead of uncaffeinated, just awakened, and scared out of her goddamn mind. "You have exactly sixty seconds to explain all this."

"Explain what, chica?" The smile was all but visible, his particular shit-eating grin. "Shoulda remembered you're in a bad mood before coffee."

How does he know? He can't know, it's six a.m. The thought that maybe Alan was somehow watching the house raised goosebumps along her arms and pooled dread in her stomach. "Thirty seconds, Alan."

"What? I'm calling to tell you to bring the kid." The way Alan said it, this was an entirely reasonable request. "Daddy wants to see Junior. Thinks maybe it'll help him get out of hock."

And I'm supposed to believe that? "You want me to bring him where?" Her gaze fastened on Vincent's.

His forehead furrowed, and he approached cautiously, leaf-light even in his heavy boots. It was unreal, how quietly he could move.

"There's a church out in Mesilla, I'll text it to you. We'll meet there and take you to el señor." Alan's tone sharpened. "Listen, where's Emilia? I keep calling, nobody's picking up."

You gave her some time off, dammit. If Cara was alone in the house, would she believe this bullshit? Maybe. Fear did funny things to you. "I don't know, Alan." She dropped her gaze, staring at the papers. If she went through them, what would she find out? Nothing she wanted to know, that was for damn sure. "I'm alone in someone else's house with a six-year-old, what am I supposed to think?"

"You called the agency?" Casually, as if it didn't matter. And why would he ask that if he thought she was just upset about Marquez getting arrested?

"Not yet." She inhaled to say *but I'm about to*, and furthermore to inform him there had been a kidnapping attempt and the cops were involved.

"Good, 'cause if you get reassigned, el señor's gonna make *me* watch the kid. I ain't no babysitter, chica." Alan laughed, and there was another sound crackling through the speaker.

Voices. Dim and muffled, but obviously male.

He wasn't alone. Why that should unnerve her so much, Cara couldn't quite figure out, but the shaking was all through her now, and every internal alarm bell she had was ringing violently, threatening to shake her into pieces. She wished she'd had time to get some coffee down before this. "Alan, this isn't right. I'm seriously weirded out here. And yesterday someone—"

"Just bring the kid to the church, and everything will be fine." The voices around him quieted, as if he was in an echoing hallway. "Señor will even pay you a bonus. You say you're all alone? Where's Emilia? where's Tomas?"

As if you don't know. But why would he lie about that?

There was no good reason, and now that she'd had some sleep and wasn't so frightened, she knew as much. "Nobody's here, Alan."

"What happened to the new guy?"

Another wrong note. Why would he care? And did he truly think her so stupid she wouldn't check the security schedule? Cara's gaze rose again to Vincent's. *Think fast.* "He vanished." The lie came naturally, instinctively. "I think he didn't like being questioned by the cops."

"Cops?" Alan swore. If he was acting, he was doing a damn good job. "They been to the house?"

"No. There was . . . Look, Alan, weird stuff is happening, and I don't like it. Where's Mr. Marquez's lawyer? Shouldn't he be—?" *Shouldn't he be calling me instead of you?*

"He'll be at the church." Alan exhaled sharply. "Listen, I gotta go, they're calling for me. Just bring the kid this afternoon, all right? Mesilla Baptist, three p.m. I'll text the address."

Then, he hung up.

Vincent stood a few steps from her, expressionless. Cara was suddenly very aware how, well, *large* he was. If he planned to do anything unpleasant, now was the time.

She set her phone down. Her mouth was full of copper fear, and she was cold. Colder than the air-conditioning. Positively arctic.

This isn't good. This isn't good at all. A roaring-rushing filled her top to bottom, as if she'd been emptied and they were pouring something carbonated into a Cara-shaped bottle.

"Hey." Vincent's voice barely reached through the ringing in her ears. "Hey, now, honey. Breathe. *Breathe.*"

I'm trying, she wanted to say. The world greyed out, then came back in a rush of color, sound, and the smell of a healthy male tinged with fabric softener on a clean shirt.

"It's okay," he said into her hair. Somehow, he had his arms around her as Cara swayed, and her cheek rested against his chest. "It's all right, sweetness. Everything's all right."

No, it's not. But Cara couldn't move. It was ridiculously comforting to have the shelter of someone else's body. Was this what Eddie felt when she hugged him?

Vincent's fingertips made small circles on her back, a soothing motion. "In and out," he said softly. "Just breathe. It's gonna be all right, sweetness. You just take that to the bank, because I'm gonna *make* it all right. Okay?"

Why would you bother? But she didn't want to ask. It was a new thing, to feel someone else taking the burden for just a moment.

This entire situation was a nightmare, but she was grateful for even a temporary, all-too-short reprieve.

WITH BREAKFAST done and his father not home, Eddie could help with the dishes. *Women's work*, Marquez called it, but Cara was of the opinion that a real man cleaned up after himself. Besides, it kept both of them occupied.

Afterward, it was time for reading and spelling, but Cara settled Eddie at the desk in the playroom with a simple writing worksheet, tracing his alphabet. It was, considering everything, an acceptable deviation from routine. "I've got to talk to Vincent in the hallway," she said, ruffling his hair.

Eddie looked up, almost dropping his chunky child's pencil. "Is he gonna leave too?"

Cara's cheeks were fever-hot. It was a completely reasonable response, she told herself, when a man had held you all the way through a panic attack and called you *sweetness*.

"I'm not going anywhere." Vincent said from the playroom door. "But I do need to talk to Ms. Cara, all right?"

"Okay." Eddie grasped his pencil and stared at the sheet with the air of a much older man resigned to paperwork.

Some things came early, Cara guessed.

She pulled the playroom door mostly shut, crossed her arms, and regarded Vince with what she hoped was a level glare and *not* the pleading stare of a woman who didn't know what the hell to do next.

"He's just a kid," she said, forestalling what she suspected he was going to suggest. There were authorities to handle this sort of thing, and he'd probably know all about them. "He's not even *my* kid, but I can't just—"

"Doesn't look like *he* knows that." Vince's expression was thoughtful, and there was a certain comfort in his looming bulk, not to mention his solidity. "Relax. You're not going to the meet."

The meet. It was security language. Something about that bothered her as well, but at the moment she was just grateful Vincent wasn't saying *Take the kid and leave him there, because I'm getting out, too.*

So Cara pushed her shoulders back, raised her chin slightly. She was all Eddie had in this fucked-up situation, and even if she was just the help, she was responsible. "I don't trust Alan as far as I can throw him. And why would he ask me to go to a church instead of . . . You know, Marquez's lawyer should be here. *Any* lawyer should be here, it's not like he can't afford them. None of this makes any *sense.*"

"Oh, it does. Just not civilian sense." Vincent eyed her for a few more moments. The side of his neck was bruised and his knuckles were scraped, but he didn't seem to care or even notice. "Let me ask you this. What are you prepared to do for this kid?"

That's the question, isn't it. It was impossible to get her back any straighter, but she tried, drawing herself up as tall as possible. Grandma Gemma, watching from heaven, would be proud indeed. "His father's an asshole." There. It was said. You weren't supposed to judge the parents, unless there was actual abuse. It was a law for this kind of work, as immutable as *Don't get attached.*

She'd broken both of them. Of course she was paying for it; that was how the world worked.

Vincent's slight shrug said he was pretty aware of Marquez's shortcomings, so to speak. "A very rich asshole who has a lot of problems right now," he said softly. "If he was able to send someone to pick up a couple packages, he would have already."

That's strange. It teased at her memory. "I don't know a lot of security-speak. What's a package?"

"Something to be picked up." One corner of his mouth curled up, and his voice dropped. It was unexpectedly intimate, standing in a hallway and whispering like this. "Or, on bodyguard duty, the person you're gonna take a bullet for."

Cara shuddered. *Not a scratch on the big package*, Alan had said into his phone. It was a hideous thought.

Just what, *exactly*, was she thinking? And should she tell Vincent about overhearing a private phone call? It could be connected, or she could simply be scared and—

"Cara?" At least he wasn't calling her *ma'am* anymore. They seemed to be past formality. "Something on your mind?"

"You mean, other than all this?" A soft, jagged laugh jolted out of her, and she found she was clutching her upper arms, digging her fingers in hard. Her knees ached, and she'd bitten the side of her tongue yesterday when her knees hit pavement. "I don't know what to do, Vincent. I'm open to suggestions."

Thankfully, he jumped right in. "Right now the best thing to do is sit tight. We know the ground here, we've got cameras and the security system. The cops might not help, but we'll know if someone's coming for us."

It was powerfully comforting to think at least *he* knew what he was doing. "The cops . . ."

Vincent's gaze was dead level, and utterly honest. "They don't seem too interested. Which isn't right."

And could mean any number of things. Cara's stomach turned over, uneasily. "I should call the agency. But what if the cops come and put Eddie in foster care? Or worse?" She took a deep breath, almost jumping when the air-conditioning ticked on and cold air rose through the registers. "When you say Marquez isn't exactly legal, what exactly do you mean?" *And are* you *a cop?*

He didn't seem like law enforcement, but that was the whole point of undercover work, right?

"You sure you want to know? Let me put it this way, I think the cops are the least of our worries." He glanced at the hallway, a quick instinctive movement, checking. Relaxed awareness poured out of him, just as comforting as his solidity. "And you told Alan I headed for the hills. Smart."

Well, thank God someone thinks I am. "I don't know why I did."

"Good instincts." A faint smile of approval curved his lips, and she couldn't look away. The corners of his eyes crinkled, and it was also powerfully comforting that he was at least her own age. "It's also a good way to tell if he's playing both sides."

Her stomach was doing a really good impression of a washing machine. "Is it?"

"Yeah." He nodded, slow and deliberate. "Because if he is, they'll try for a home snatch tonight, thinking you're here alone."

That wasn't it. I think I just didn't want to get you into any trouble. Cara turned this over inside her head; Eddie needed her to make the right decision—and not just so she'd keep her job.

No. To keep him safe. That was the largest consideration here, the one all others had to take backseat to. "Maybe we shouldn't be here."

"You got a place to go? With the kid? A friend, family, anything?"

Not really. And she suspected he wouldn't be asking if *he* had someone to call. He seemed the loner type.

"My stuff's in storage since I'm a resident nanny. My parents and grandmother are gone, I don't have other family." Ben would be worse than useless; besides, *divorce* was a two-way street. "My friends . . ." Other nannies wouldn't want anything to do with this. They had their own jobs to think of, and another host family would be on the phone to the cops and their own lawyers in a hot minute. Cara wouldn't blame them, either. "There's nobody." Her conscience pricked at her, hard. "Look, if you've got someplace to go, I won't hold it against you. This is more than you signed up for." He probably hadn't even been paid yet.

Or had he? It really, really sucked to be suspecting the only other person in the rowboat with you during a disaster. She didn't know a single thing about this man.

Her cheeks were *still* hot. For God's sake, did she have to *blush*, too? It was a final indignity.

"I'm not going anywhere." His chin set stubbornly, and he rubbed at his cheek with blunt callused fingertips. "Seems like a stranger's the only one you can trust right now."

Except she had only his word he was a stranger, and not one of Alan's friends. "I guess," she hedged. He'd fought off the kidnappers—why call them anything else?—and held her in the kitchen, rubbing her back and saying exactly what she needed to hear, his voice rumbling under her cheekbone.

"I can tell you don't, though. That's good." Vincent took a step back, giving her plenty of space. "I'll keep an eye on everything from the camera room. Stay in the house. Don't answer the phone. I'll do it."

Was there a difference between being in a fortress or a prison? You couldn't leave a prison.

It was looking like she couldn't leave here, either. Not without Eddie.

Cara nodded. "Okay." For now, she'd let him call the shots. It was yet another unexpected, uneasy relief.

Clicking Along

THE PHONE RANG at odd intervals during the long, syrup-slow, sunny afternoon. The house stood silent and secretive, the heat pump keeping its interior cave-chilly, sprinklers outside chugging when the timers told them to open the sluices. Vincent stared at the monitors, thinking.

His own cell phone sat in front of him, a wafer-thin black brick with its shockproof holder. Once or twice he picked it up and thumbed to Klemp's number, then set it down, the screen going dark after a prescribed period.

He needed backup if half of what he suspected was true, but dragging Klemp into this wouldn't do the other man any favors. Besides, Klemp had put him onto the job—did he know Alan?

There were one or two other buddies he could call. Hell, he could get the whole squad out—except for Klemp, who would be furious to be left out of the loop, but Vince could say it was because of his leg. None of the others would mind, especially Tax or Jackson, but the situation was far too fluid.

Marquez could still show up, angry but only out whatever cash he'd had to post for bail. And though Vince had put all the papers back, it would still be clear someone had rifled through them.

It was an uncomfortable thought. There were even more uncomfortable thoughts to be had from the file folder full of news clippings about the death of Amelia Marquez, survived by a son and a husband. Tucked right next to it was a folder with two glossy surveillance eight-by-tens of Cara, not to mention a pretty thorough background check on her. On the one hand, of course a proud papa would do his own homework on the woman taking care of his son.

On the other, it also looked like Marquez had plans. Or a really big birthday wish.

At least Cara was for real. She was probably the only thing in this scenario that was exactly what it appeared to be. Well, her and the kid.

The poor kid.

Vince did *not* like where this was going. Staying put was the best move at the moment, but that would change in a hurry if professionals came to pick up a couple of unprotected packages. The boy was easy; they could even pump a couple slugs into the nanny and vanish with a tiny six-year-old probably limp from shock.

His fists clenched every time he considered the notion.

The kid was busy arranging a few divisions' worth of Hot Wheels in color and size-coded lines on the playroom floor. Cara had her yoga mat out, and was probably getting rid of yesterday's aches and pains. It boggled the mind how she could stretch herself into a pretzel with such determination.

So far Eddie seemed to consider this a holiday, and she was keeping up that same fragile, brittle calm. The only break was her trembling in his arms near the coffeemaker, and he could still feel the exact spot where her cheek had rested, smell the fragrance of her messy dark hair. The shaking had gone down bit by bit, and when she stepped away he had to force himself not to drag her back.

It had felt so goddamn stupidly *right.*

Now, balanced on her mat, she spread her arms, chin level, front knee bent. He could almost hear her slight exhalation. Eddie's head craned; he was talking to her.

Eyes closed, Cara answered, probably some soothing words. What was she thinking about?

That's not the question. The question is, what the hell are you *thinking, Vince? This can go sideways in a heartbeat. You should drag her out of here. Leave the kid, he's baggage.*

That was the thought an absolute bastard would have. And she wouldn't go for it, no sir. What decent woman would leave a kid behind, especially one she'd been looking after for months?

At least she'd told Alan that Vince had taken a powder. Smart of her; there was probably more going on behind those big dark eyes than Vincent could ever guess.

No use denying he wanted a crack at it. He wanted to get to know her a little better, and maybe, just maybe—

A flicker of motion in his peripheral vision brought his head around. The gate cams were still going, two rovers and a stationary.

A white sedan crept close to the gate. Vincent's skin chilled, the old *get ready to tango but not quite yet* feeling pouring down his back like melting ice. The car rolled to a stop just outside camera range; a quarter-turn would show him the plate number—or at least a fuzzy facsimile. If he was really curious, he could make one of the moving cameras swing around; the manual override was right there.

But that would tell them someone was looking. Vincent glanced at his watch, noting the time. Sunset coming up.

The car sat for a few minutes, idling. Someone could have gotten out up the street and hopped the fence, but he didn't think so. They might be wondering if Cara really was at the house, and if so, why she wasn't picking up. Three o'clock had come and gone, and since she'd missed the meet, Alan would maybe think she was sitting in a cop shop spilling her guts, maybe with some of Marquez's paperwork.

If Vince hadn't been around, she probably would have. And that was a bad idea if even half of what he suspected was going on. CPS would swoop in to snap up Eddie, though, and she couldn't bear that thought.

The lady was a marshmallow, and it was going to get her killed. Fortunately, Vincent wasn't a civilian, and he was on the job.

The doc would probably find me clicking right along now. Funny how that worked. Give a man a task and he settled right in.

Only it wasn't the job settling him. It was the feeling burning in his arms and the warm spot on his chest, and the way he'd been able to calm her down. A few strokes, a few nonsense words, and it left a man feeling like a hero when she stepped away and raised her chin, all right again, pale but with red blotches high on her cheeks, signal flags on a pair of objectives.

Hero's just a word for someone who gets everyone else killed, Sparky had been fond of saying. *Better to just do your damn job.*

Vince studied the car. Just like watching an enemy encampment from cover, barely even breathing despite knowing you were safe. A single twitch could give you away, a glitter of binocs, anything.

"Come on," he muttered. "Show me something, assholes. Knock on the door and ask to play, I'm begging you."

The car backed up, slowly. Just a mistake, the wrong address, no harm no foul. It edged out of sight and Vincent scanned the outside monitors, alert for any twitch that shouldn't be there. They couldn't be planning a home invasion right now, not with all the civilians coming home for dinner. It would be unprofessional, but worse than that, it would be flat-out stupid.

Finally, there was nothing left to see. Even the wind had died down; branches hung motionless. The sprinklers clicked off. Cara had finished her stretching and now sat on the floor next to Eddie, listening while he lifted up one car after another, eager for her approval.

I know the feeling, kid.

That settled it. He needed a nap; now he knew and his pulse dropped, his breathing evened out, the world was nice and simple, just the way he liked it.

If he was right, it would happen tonight. If he wasn't, in the morning they'd move anyway.

THE KITCHEN WAS well-stocked, and Eddie helped make the tortillas. It wasn't bad, even if they were a little lumpy. Vincent ate without tasting rice, canned beans somehow made into something other than paste-nuggets, shredded beef, salad, sour cream, cheese. He was fueling for the night's potential games, but he had to slow down when Eddie elbowed him—or tried to.

The kid couldn't quite reach.

"Use your napkin," Eddie stage-whispered, wiping at a dab of sour cream on his own hands. "Or she gets mad."

"I don't get mad," Cara said from the sink, her back to both of them. Today she was in jeans and a soft pink scoop-neck instead of a dress. It was just as good, especially when he could glance at how lovingly the denim cupped her hips. "But yes, napkins are an essential, Eddie. Thanks for reminding our guest."

"He ain't a guest." Eddie grinned at him, an expression of broad good will. Looked like the kid was in a mischievous mood.

"Eddie." A single word, soft and sweet, but with an undertone of warning. Cara rinsed her hands; Vince hoped the water heater wasn't turned up all the way. He'd almost boiled himself this morning, a welcome change from cold camp showers.

"Sorry," the kid mumbled, and put his head down.

"It's all right," Vincent said quietly. Getting on Eddie's good side might even turn out to be simple. "I'm not using my manners either. She'll be mad at us both."

"I can hear you, you know." Cara sighed. She wrung out a dishcloth, draped it over the faucet's hood.

"Come and eat." Was he actually trying to cajole? Wonders never ceased. He couldn't bark at her to *get your fucking gut filled so you don't bitch off in combat*, though. She wasn't a soldier. "You'll need it."

"Maybe she's afraid of getting fat." Eddie took a huge forkful of rice, gave it a token chew, and down it went. He ate like a man just back from a long, nerve-wracking patrol. "Girls are like that."

Oh, buddy. Vincent almost choked on a mouthful of beans. *You just stepped on a land mine.* "Uh, kid—"

"No dessert for you." But Cara actually sounded amused, and she found a perch on Eddie's other side, settling with sweet, natural grace. "You need some more cheese, kiddo?"

"No, I got plenty." But Eddie was watching Vincent closely. "I like him now," he announced with a sharp nod, like a scientist discovering a good experiment's results. "He doesn't get mad."

Now who *could* get mad at a six-year-old? Only an asshole. And while Vince was a sonofabitch himself, he wasn't a dick. Or at least, he tried not to be.

"I'm glad you've changed your mind." Cara stared at her plate like it held slop rather than beautifully arranged rice, beans, salad, and shredded beef left over from another meal and carefully stored in the fridge. She even diced tomatoes perfectly.

How did anyone learn to do *that*?

For a moment, Vince let himself think about it. Not a big pile like this faux adobe bullshit but maybe a trim, yellow-painted two story, or a ranch-style if she didn't like stairs. Coming home, setting his shit down by the front door, and the kid running from somewhere to give him a hug. A dinner on the stove and a dark-haired woman smiling as she set plates on a table, and knowing that once the kid was in bed he could slide a hand around her nape and murmur something nice, something that would make her lips curve and her eyes dance.

It was a good thought, a little fantasy he could unfold and pore over when he was in-country, sleeping God only knew where and eating God only knew what, with the filth and the blood and the death lurking in every corner. Nobody had to know that's what he was thinking about.

Especially not an innocent kid and a woman who probably wouldn't have looked at him twice if he hadn't been basically forced on her. Only a real creep would be thinking about using the uncertainty and the danger to get her a little closer.

To get himself inside that shelter, even temporarily.

"You should eat," he repeated, harshly. "We're getting out of here in the morning."

Eddie perked up, swinging his legs. His shoes flashed, little lights in the heels winking like ship signals. "Where we going?"

"Someplace they can't find us." Cara picked up her fork, staring mournfully at her plate. "Do you have enough milk?"

"Does that mean you're my Mami now?" Eddie swung his legs,

clearly excited at the notion. The back door's glass upper half was full of ruby sunset, a bloody warning. "Because—"

"Let her eat." Vincent didn't miss the way the kid gave him a long, considering look, probably gauging how much further he could push it. "We're taking care of you right now, Eddie. You don't need to worry about anything else. Worrying's our job."

"Oh." But it was Cara the six-year-old looked to, his eyebrows up and anxiety printed on his little face.

"He's right." What did it cost her to smile, pushing her shoulders back and taking a forkful of rice? The light was kind to her, burnishing her cheeks and glowing in her hair. "Worrying is a big person's job, Eddie. Let us do it."

"Does Dad ever worry?" Eddie swung his legs again, his toes just touching the cabinet.

I'll bet wherever he is now, he's plenty worried. "I'm sure he does." Vincent tried not to sound grim. "Eat up, buddy. If we've got to move, it's best on a full stomach." It would—hopefully—be years before the kid found out how right that little truism was.

Decades, even.

"I don't walk with my *stomach*," Eddie said, somewhat pompously. "I use my *feet*."

Vincent's laughter surprised him. Maybe it surprised Cara too, because she gave him a startled, extraordinary look, her dark eyes still and thoughtful, before she laughed too.

He liked the way the two streams sounded running together, and when Eddie giggled, not getting the joke but happy to be included, it sounded . . .nice.

Real nice. At least until Vincent remembered what was likely to come down the road tonight.

After dinner, it would be time to suit up.

Overspent on Decibel

VINCENT INSISTED she pack for her and Eddie after dinner. She made it a game, as if they were going on vacation, and Eddie was thrilled at the idea.

One bag, Vincent said, that faraway look in his dark eyes. *Light enough for you to carry both if you have to. Change of clothes, couple toiletries, your paperwork. One bag is all you get, so don't get fancy.* Here he'd paused, looking thoughtful. *And some shoes for the kid that don't light up, okay?*

She was surprised he'd noticed Eddie's beloved blinking sneakers, but maybe she shouldn't be. Vincent seemed very . . .detail-oriented.

In a little while, she'd get up and steal into Eddie's bedroom, just to make sure he was breathing. And also to settle next to his bed again. For now, though, Cara lay on her back, her hands resting loosely on her belly. Her eyes were closed, but she still saw it—the spreading stain on the sheet, the crimson blotches of bloody slurry, Ben's pale, bearded face after she'd finished sobbing against his shoulder in the hospital room.

It's actually kind of a relief . . .

Cara stirred, uneasily. The agency warned against getting too attached. It wasn't fair to the kids.

Nothing's fair. You know that.

She couldn't just leave Eddie. If Marquez came back, what were her options? Inform him that he was a shitty father right before she waltzed out the door and onto another assignment? She didn't *have* to do this, she had her MFA, her savings, good references from at least two accountants, and work waiting elsewhere. This job was just a way of coping with her own issues, and *that* made her just as selfish as Eddie's father.

At least Marquez was openly a bad parent. She was a silent danger, masquerading as a real mother. Wasn't that worse? What had she been *thinking*?

You were thinking someone else's kid wouldn't die on you, Cara. If, that is, you were thinking at all.

How bad was it to use a six-year-old as therapy? She'd judge someone else for doing it, and harshly, too. Next to Vincent's quiet dedication to a pair of strangers, she was feeling a sorry beast indeed.

Her fingers tensed, digging in. Her own treacherous body couldn't be trusted—it had, after all, mercilessly flushed a new life out on a tide of blood—and neither could her feelings. Neither could her *mind.*

What was there to trust in this fucked-up situation? She should have called the agency well before now, but she was selfish. A big old pile of selfish shit.

This is getting you nowhere. She rolled onto her side, pushed herself up. Gathered her pillow and the top blanket, a yawn filling her mouth and reaching down her throat. Sleeping on the floor was uncomfortable, but it was only what she deserved.

Still, it wasn't right for her to possibly disturb Eddie because she needed some kind of comfort.

Late at night, there was absolutely nothing that could save you from the tiny, hairy, sharp-toothed doubt in your own head. Cara hunched over the pillow, cuddling it close to her stomach, and stared at her slightly open door.

She might have spent some serious time sitting and brooding, but an earsplitting klaxon punched the air, forcing her off the bed and into a crouch with her hands clapped over her ears and an unheard scream vibrating in her throat before she realized it was the burglar alarm.

Looked like Marquez had overspent on decibels as well as the rest of the house. But why was it so *loud*? The klaxon was supposed to be directional, louder near the . . .

Near whatever circuit, window or door, had been broken.

Eddie's window had bars, but maybe he'd crept out of bed to open it as he sometimes did, and maybe Vincent had armed the entire system instead of just the regular bits. The poor kid would be terrified by sudden noise. Cara scrambled to her feet, almost tripping over the dropped blanket, and ran for her door.

Afterward, she could never quite remember the whole event, just tiny, disconnected snippets. Lights flashed, partly because her eyelids were fluttering and partly because the security alarm unit on the wall was strobing as well as emitting its wail. The playroom was its regular nighttime self, but there was a shadow in Eddie's bedroom door—big, hulking, and male, in dark clothing. For a moment she thought it was Vincent, then she realized it wasn't tall enough.

And even through the noise, she heard Eddie's piping, terrified scream.

Cara didn't stop to think. She simply launched herself at the intruder.

EDDIE'S WINDOW was slightly open, solid bars still standing sentinel. The curtains fluttered on the exhalation of a desert night; Eddie was kicking and screaming, his face a mask of terror as a broad-shouldered, monstrous shadow lifted him. Weird goggles turned the kidnapper's shape into a nightmare caricature, and Cara's body moved with thoughtless speed, almost knocking over the second man moving in from the door. She was past him in a trice, throwing herself onto the first man's back.

A stunning impact clipped the side of her head, the world turned over, and a hot slick spattering touched the wall, dripped down her face. Cara found herself on the floor, but her body knew what to do and sprang up like a jack in the box.

Oh hell no, she thought. *No you don't.*

The world somersaulted again, because the man in the door *hit* her. Cara went sprawling; the first man lifted Eddie like a sack of potatoes and yelled something. She could see his mouth moving. Both of them were in funny black security gear and goggles; the thought that this was the police and maybe she shouldn't be fighting vanished when Eddie's little arms flailed.

Son of a bitch. Fury ignited in her belly, and Cara leapt up again. She didn't realize she was screaming, too.

"*You leave my baby alone!*"

The man in the door had a short black stick, and he raised it. She knew it was going to hit, knew it was going to hurt—and she didn't care.

All she cared about was Eddie. She flung herself at the first man again, and the black stick—a baton, she realized, though it didn't look like the ones Grandma had always talked about spinning in high school—reached its apex.

Then it began to descend.

Passable Job

OF COURSE THE trouble would come while he was on patrol at the other end of the house, checking a likely break-in spot.

All the same, he had to hand it to the woman. She had guts.

Vincent tapped the man's knee from behind and got his fingers in the helmet straps; a quick twist, an unheard *snap,* and the fucker went limp, spilling to the floor. The strobe lights were a nuisance and the siren was too; he ignored both and stepped into Eddie's bedroom. It was a big space, but seemed crowded now with one asshole in tac gear on the floor and the other trying to heft a six-year-old while Cara, her hair flying and her tank top torn, seemed bound and determined to get herself laid out.

Or worse.

She tripped over the now-sprawling guy near the door and went down hard; he wanted to catch her, but the asshole holding Eddie had priority. The thought that he could let them take the kid since he was obviously their primary target appeared and disappeared in a flash.

Cara wouldn't give the time of day to a man who let these jackasses take her Eddie. And what the hell, Vince liked the little boy too.

Liked him a lot.

So it was a short shot to the side of the snatcher's head; the goggles, no matter how expensive, were more a nuisance than a help inside a residence. With Eddie struggling, the motherfucker was off-balance and Vincent tapped his knee too, forcing it in a direction it wasn't designed for. The man's mouth opened—he had nice teeth, clearly a well-nourished soldier—in a soundless scream, and he went over, almost landing on the kid. Vince's hands arrived just in time; he snatched Eddie away and kicked the would-be kidnapper, heavy boots sinking into ribs just where the vest's front armor ended. If you could get a steel-capped toe in there it would do a lot of good, and Vince tried to put enough force behind the strike to drive a soccer ball through a concrete wall.

It was unexpectedly satisfying. Eddie was in a paroxysm of fear, struggling until Vince got his arms fully around the kid and hugged him, ignoring the small fist clipping his ear. It hurt, but not badly. "*Calm down!*" he shouted. "*It's me!*"

Eddie went limp and Vincent dumped him on the bed for safekeeping, turning on his heel. Cara lay very still, almost draped over the guy at the door.

If he hurt her, I'll kill him again. He lifted a boot, brought it down squarely on the kidnapper's chest, repeated the move. Two strikes, hopefully he'd broken a few ribs. He was about to give the guy a heel to his throat when the sound and strobing lights died between one whoop and the next. Cara twitched, sliding off the corpse with painful, boneless fluidity. Eddie was sobbing, great sucking gasps of air, and for a moment, there was a terrifying, vertiginous certainty that Cara was slipping free because her body no longer had anyone in it.

No. No, goddammit, no. "Cara." He was on his knees next to her with a jolt, not quite realizing how he'd gotten there. "Oh, fuck. Cara. No."

She twitched, rolling onto her side. Relief burst through him even though blood painted the side of her face, black in the uncertain light. The alarm wasn't braying now; he had to think of why. It was a six-man team, if he guessed their actual entry point right, and it would have been enough to overwhelm a girl and a child.

Had whoever was running this exercise *really* been stupid enough to think Vince was gone?

Her eyes opened, terribly wide and senseless, dark holes in a pale face. Her lips twitched. *Of course. They cut the power, probably the landline too.* Figuring that out wasn't the relief it could have been, because it should have been his first thought.

"Eddie?" Cara whispered.

The kid scrambled off the bed, almost tripped over his attacker, and darted past Vincent to throw his arms around her, sobbing.

Vincent sagged. This breather was short-lived. Four intruders left, possibly more if anyone had two brain cells and figured out Vince might not leave the two civilians just lying around for collection.

He didn't have eyes on any intruders at the moment. Which meant he had to get his packages moving. "Get up," he whispered fiercely. "Eddie, get your shoes on. Let's go."

Then Vincent heard movement in the dark, and it wasn't theirs.

BOTH CIVILIANS tried their best to stay quiet, and did a passable job for two of the untrained. Vincent took point, straining his ears; if they got out of here without a fight it would be a miracle. The best exit was the kitchen, but the attackers' primary point of entry had to be through there and the garage. Cara was moving gingerly, but nothing was broken and she didn't appear to be in shock yet.

Yet being, of course, the operative word.

Both of them had backpacks, filled right after dinner; their go-clothes had been laid out just as Vincent wanted. Pajama-clad Eddie scrubbed at his face with his free hand, trying to keep the gulping sobs down; his tiny sneakers didn't have LEDs in the heels and his navy hoodie was almost too small for him but just the right shade to keep him hidden at night. Cara, in workout pants and a flannel over her tank top, didn't shush the boy. She simply held his hand and pulled him into her hip whenever they halted.

Vince kept the gun low. If he was lucky, they'd get out of here without traumatizing either civilian further.

Fat chance.

He beckoned them across the hall. Cara was a dream, she stayed right where he put her each time they stopped. Blood dripped into his eyes, a tacky-wet irritation; his ribs ached. He didn't remember one of the assholes in Eddie's room clipping him, but it was like that when the adrenaline started. He'd feel it after he had a chance to sleep, along with the bruises on his shoulder and his split, puffing knuckles.

Tomorrow would be uncomfortable. Right now, though, all he felt was the fierce, cold concentration of moving in enemy territory.

It happened right where he thought it would, at the entry to the sunken den with its huge, circular, glass-sheathed fake fireplace. He expected them to hit from the side as soon as he stepped through, and he was ready except for the bastard coming from the left instead of right.

They were good, but they weren't professionals. They went for the gun instead of the man, which was only necessary or applicable in certain situations. It would've gotten them one of Sparky Lee's withering looks and a few push-ups to break them of the habit.

Vincent let the man push through, spinning aside; the silenced gun barked twice and the fuckhead dropped like a ton of bricks. The enemy couldn't shoot without harming the packages and that was outside their parameters—or so he hoped, letting momentum carry him down and behind a curved leather couch. Someone cursed, a low electric oath, and Cara gasped. Eddie made a tiny noise like he'd been hit, and Vince *almost* burst up out of cover to clean out whoever had dared touch either of them.

Simple logic, as well as training, kept him moving in the opposite direction. He was a bigger threat than two civilians, and the hostiles had night-vision gear. He surged up and crashed into another, a warm living bulk sensed more than seen, his pupils stretched wide to catch any glimmer. There was a wicked little gleam, a keen edge parting air, and he locked the man's knife wrist, a half-turn and his center of gravity dropping. He surged forward, and they hit the glass over the fireplace.

Crash. Vincent let go just before they hit, his arms windmilling to shed momentum, and whatever god looked after drunks, small children, and the blindly protective dealt him a break.

He didn't go onto the jagged, broken spears. He almost fell sideways, remembered there was a sharp-edged chrome and glass table there, and dropped instead into a crouch, one hand out and blindly groping.

Silence, except for his own deep fast breathing and Eddie's thin, choked sob.

"It's all right," Cara whispered in the dark. "It's okay, Eddie. I'm here, I'm not going to let anything happen to you."

Which meant Vince couldn't either. Where were the last two? He shut his eyes for a moment, thinking furiously.

They've got to have transport. Makes sense for them to peel off toward the garage, both to cover the initial entry point and to catch the civvies if they head for the car. Is someone watching the cameras—no, power's out, don't have to worry about that.

Everything else was a chance he'd have to take. He straightened, his back roughening as he broke cover. "Around the room," he said softly, "to the left. Careful, broken glass."

"Okay."

His two packages blundered along. There were shelves of high-priced curios arranged with plenty of designer-approved space between them; something fell and broke with a tinkle.

"*Shit*," Cara hissed, and Vincent's face felt strange. Blood dripped from his chin, and he was smiling.

At least, until he heard the man in the broken glass shift and groan. He ached to pop a couple into the body to make sure, but Cara and Eddie had almost reached the short hall leading past Marquez's office to the back door.

Almost there. He didn't say it out loud, that was the surest way to make everything go sideways again. Still, he could think it all he wanted.

Just like he could imagine her smiling in a small yellow house all he wanted. It was a good image, and he held onto it as he checked the hall.

Normal

THE DAY'S HEAT had long since leached away, and Cara shivered as they plunged into dry, crackling shrubbery. There was only one place along the wall girdling Marquez's estate that didn't have glass or metal spikes, and—true to form—Vincent knew exactly where it was. "You go up first." He made a quick movement, holstering a gun Cara didn't want to think about. The silencer, unscrewed with quick, habitual movements, had vanished somewhere too. "Then I'll hand Eddie up."

That's great, except how will we get down? Branches poked at her side, her eyes refused to focus quite right, and her old black sneakers were wet from the sprinklers' midnight bathing. "Okay," she managed, and blinked furiously.

"Good girl." Warm approval filled his voice, but he wasn't looking at her. A few specks of streetlamp light plunged over the wall and managed to slip through leathery leaves, and he was watching the vast expanse of well-watered lawn. The swimming pool was a black blot instead of brilliant blue, and no golden squares or slices shone from the house.

"It's so dark," she breathed, then shook her head. Of course it was dark, it was night and the power was out.

"They cut the lights too late." Vincent bent, interlacing his fingers to make a cup for her feet. If he was hurt, he gave no indication. He was so damn *calm*, she almost wanted to shake him. "Should have done it before the alarm sounded."

"What triggered the alarm?" She felt blindly for the wall, meaning to brace herself before he lifted her. Suddenly, it seemed impossible. Her legs trembled, and her arms were wet noodles. "Where were you?"

"Motion detector." Vincent didn't shrug, he just half-crouched, his hands ready. "I had them pointing at likely places. Didn't think they'd be stupid enough to keep the power on, though. I was patrolling the other place they could have come in. Go on up, sweetness."

Oh, God. Not sure I can. But for Eddie, she had to try.

The little boy didn't want to let go of her, and the feeling was emphatically mutual. She had to murmur a few quiet reassurances before Eddie's hands loosened, and as soon as Cara was perched on the wall, Vincent lifted the boy and his backpack, a small but awkward parcel. Maybe that's why bodyguards called people *packages.*

Eddie's mouth worked in the dimness, his lips trembling, and his eyes were huge.

"It's all right," she whispered. "It's going to be okay. I'm here."

"Stay right there." It took Vincent two tries to reach the top of the wall; he ignored her outstretched hand and used a few sturdy branches to lever himself up with a grunt. He dropped on the other side, a jolt that made her wince in sympathy, and she lowered Eddie into his waiting arms.

Streetlamp glow painted the side of Vince's face with black ink. It was blood, and Cara's stomach cramped furiously. She tasted copper; her teeth had cut the inside of her cheek. Eddie had a few drops and smears on his face, but none of it was his, thank God.

Cara half-fell into Vincent's arms. He was still solid, and only made a slight *huff* sound when he took her weight. She slid down his body, slowly, and he set her on her squishing feet.

"Okay," he said, and glanced both ways. "There's a ditch at the corner, we're aiming for that. You got your backpacks? Good job, soldiers. Let's move."

We're not soldiers. "You're hurt." Her voice outright quivered. Eddie stared up at her; his gaze swiveled over to Vincent. The kid looked terrified. She didn't blame him, but now she felt like an idiot, too. Calling attention to their wounds wasn't going to calm anyone down.

"It's superficial." Vincent beckoned. "We've got to go."

Why aren't we taking the car? There must be a reason. Cara nodded, trying to look like she understood all this. His calm was absurdly comforting, until she realized *she* probably looked just as calm to little, clinging Eddie.

And looks were deceiving, because she was scared stiff.

The ditch was right where he said it would be, dry as a bone since it wasn't flash-flood season just yet. Cara thought of snakes and shuddered, but Vincent moved ahead confidently, half-bent. He stopped only once, when the sound of an engine approached; he lifted one bent arm with a fist and Cara crouched, unsure of what the signal meant. Eddie leaned against her, his throat working as he swallowed, and his eyelids fluttered sleepily.

Vincent waited for what felt like forever after the car sped away, taking the slight rise onto Holyoke Street. Then he beckoned them along again.

The ditch ended near a cul-de-sac of smaller, much less expensive homes, and he led them to a black Land Rover that sat obediently in a pool of shadow between two lights, as if someone was visiting the neighborhood overnight and hadn't known quite where to park. The Rover's lights flashed as they approached and she jumped nervously, but it was only the doors unlocking. Vincent tugged open the one behind the driver's side and his teeth gleamed, a startlingly wide, white grin even though the dome light didn't come on. "In you go. Good job. You did great. Especially you, Eddie. That was really good."

He can't possibly mean that. And where the hell did this car come from? It wasn't time to look a gift horse in the mouth, so to speak. Still . . . "Where did this come from?"

"It's mine, I moved it down here this afternoon." Vincent glanced over her shoulder, a brief scanning flicker. "Eddie, your booster's in there."

"I never would have thought of that," Cara muttered. "You're amazing."

"Glad you think so." He still didn't look at her, just at the street. If he was nervous, he was still doing a damn good job of hiding it, and she decided she'd better hurry.

As soon as she clambered in, Vincent shut the door, and all the starch went out of her arms and legs at once.

A HALF HOUR LATER, Eddie was in a Golden Motel bathtub as warm water ran, splashing his yellow plastic duck on the waves and yawning hugely. Cara dabbed at the nasty slice along Vincent's hairline with a cotton ball soaked in peroxide. "You thought of everything." Her voice didn't want to work quite right, and neither did her fingers. They both shook just the tiniest bit.

"Trained for it." Vincent's eyes half-lidded, and there were dark semicircles underneath. He looked about as tired as she felt. He wouldn't let her attend his bleeding head until her own wound—a tiny, finger-tip-long cut near her hairline she absolutely didn't remember getting—was disinfected and painted with liquid bandage. Eddie didn't have a scratch on him, but he was probably going to have nightmares for the rest of his life.

Just the thought weighed her down with lead blankets. She blinked furiously, trying to clear her head, and focused on her work.

"Did you kill him?" Eddie piped up, smacking his duck on the water's surface. "The bad guy, did you kill him?"

Vincent's mouth turned down at the corners, but he kept looking at her. Apparently, Cara had to deal with *this* particular battle.

"Wash up," she said, firmly. Thank goodness she sounded like she knew what she was doing; it was bad advertising, but she'd take it. "With the soap, but not your hair, okay?"

"But I want to know if he *kilt* them," Eddie plainly considered this the most important part of the night's events. He sloshed to the side of the tub and draped his arms along it, clutching the duck. "He fell down. Went boom."

"They're alive," Vincent said heavily, and Cara knew it was a lie. What else could he say to a six-year-old? "But they won't come after you again, Eddie. Do what she says."

What happens next? Her hands shook; there was a small mountain of cotton balls and tissues stained varying shades of crimson on the counter. She reached for the small glass container of liquid bandage Vincent had produced; it was nose-stinging acrid like nail polish and burned like acid. He'd even thought of first-aid, though the prospect of an injury the kit couldn't cover was very large, very real, and utterly terrifying now that she had some time to think.

"Bad guys." Eddie nodded sagely. "Like in the movies."

Oh, God. She swallowed the urge to scream. Vincent's hands came up, folding around hers and the glass bottle. He was warm, solid, and very gentle.

"Breathe, sweetness." He had good eyelashes—not as thick as Eddie's, but a casual observer would probably think the two of them related. Their coloring was almost the same. "You've got the shakes. It's normal."

Nothing about this is normal. Cara could find no answer, in all the words she knew, for that statement.

"Is she gonna throw up?" Eddie bounced, splashing, suddenly very interested in this turn of events.

"Turn the water off." Vincent's hands were warm and gentle, calluses scraping her knuckles. "Now."

Eddie did.

Vincent's gaze trapped hers. Eyes were windows to the soul, certainly, but she couldn't figure out what she was seeing in his. His chin tipped up; the thought that the same hands cupping hers so gently had also taken someone's life set off another round of trembling. "You're both gonna spool down when the adrenaline crash hits," he said. "Don't fight it. Best thing is to sleep. It's a buffer."

Did they teach you that in the Army? Or some other branch? Now wasn't a good time to ask. "Okay."

His gaze fastened on her mouth, and for some reason, that made her nervous.

"You'll want to clean up too," he continued, "as soon as the little guy's done. I've got some protein bars. You eat a little bit, brush your teeth, go to sleep. In the morning it'll be like a dream."

"More like a nightmare," she whispered.

"Maybe." He nodded slightly, like she'd said something profound. "But it'll be over, that's the important thing. And now you know."

"What?" *What exactly do I know, now?* Pretty much all she could figure out was they were in a hotel, they'd paid cash, she and Eddie were entirely at this man's mercy, and someone was dead. Or maybe even more than one person was, and how on earth was she supposed to deal with that?

How was *Eddie* supposed to deal with it?

"I'm not going to let anything happen to you." Vincent's gaze swung up from her mouth, found hers again. "Ever."

Eddie clung to the side of the tub, watching solemnly. What would his father think of this?

I don't care, she realized. Her kid was safe, that was the important thing. All three of them were alive. It could so easily have turned out differently. She cleared her throat, uncomfortably aware of her cheeks heating up again. Was blushing a natural response to almost getting kidnapped twice?

Nobody had ever looked at her this way. Nobody had ever fought off armed attackers in front of her before, either. There were new experiences all over the place.

Maybe the agency should put that in their recruitment brochures.

"Okay." She nodded. Vincent's hands tensed, then slid away reluctantly. He kept watching her face while she finished cleaning his scrapes, and didn't flinch when she painted the stinging, nasty liquid stuff on.

It was only later, when he was in the shower and Eddie curled into her side on one of the room's double beds, sleep claiming him almost instantly, that she realized the most obvious thing of all.

Vincent's going to get killed if this keeps up. Then, an even more terrifying thought arrived, welling up from the deep place behind his eyes she'd stared into, unable to name what she saw.

He might even want to.

But she passed out all at once, like a light switch flicking, just as he'd said she would.

Knife to a Gunfight

A BRIGHT HOT morning dawned, but there were black smudges over the distant mountains. Flood season was coming, summer breaking into long sharp pieces, and a dry uncertain wind sent dust devils skipping and dancing across parking lots and back roads.

Also, Cara's cell phone, retained despite the risk of tracking because Vince was betting they weren't dealing with true professionals, held two messages from Alan and one from the nanny agency.

The latter was routine, according to her; they checked in once a month and took a report. The messages from Alan, on the other hand, were *not.* By any stretch of the imagination.

Chica, you better bring the boy, or el señor's gonna think you're kidnapping him. Church of the Holy Assumption out in Mesilla. I sent you the address, come on. Tomorrow, one p.m. I can't keep el señor happy much longer . . .Cara, it's Alan. Come on, pick up your phone. Talk to me. Bring little Eduardo to meet his daddy, all right? Do the right thing here.

Either he thought she was stupid, or he was betting on her being scared enough to grab at any offer of safety, no matter how unlikely. Or, more possibly, he was covering his own ass in case any law enforcement someone rich and amoral didn't own—if there were any left in the US—got a crack at Cara's messages.

Vince was willing to bet it was a combination of all three, actually.

"I still think we should go to the cops," Cara said softly. Her hair glowed under strong golden light, a cloud of stubborn curls; she kept glancing nervously through the half-open bathroom door. Eddie sprawled luxuriously on the double bed the two civvies had shared, clicking through TV channels with the air of a kid well-satisfied with life. "Or the agency's legal arm. There's got to be *something.*"

Vincent strangled a flare of impatience. "That's a really bad idea," he repeated, tilting his head slightly to stretch his cervical muscles. He'd stiffened up; it wasn't bad, but a few more nights like the last and his performance would degrade. "The cops didn't do anything when the kid almost got snatched in a parking lot, what are they gonna do now?"

"This is a little different." Her chin jutted a little, stubbornly, and it was official. She was beautiful even when borderline sulky.

Except sulky was the wrong word. He couldn't think of the right one with her standing so close. She even smelled good, clean and fresh though all she had to work with was motel soap.

Vince had to drag his mind back to business. He'd stiffened up overnight but not badly, and the bathroom's close confines were miraculously getting rid of the rest of his aches. Or, more precisely, replacing them with a different set, spurred by the woman close enough to almost, *almost* touch.

"Do you really want to try to explain this to them?" He sounded harsh, and a bright jet of loathing went through him at high speed before vanishing.

It would distract him, and he needed all his focus right now.

"We didn't do anything wrong." But the frightened little gleam far back in Cara's dark eyes said she didn't believe it. What else did good girls do but run to the teacher or the cops? She was a rule-follower, like most civilians.

"Yeah, forensics will bear us out at the scene. But I don't want to be sitting in stockade while they grind through paperwork and you're unprotected, okay?" He took a deep breath, repeated the mission again. "It's really simple. I'll go to the church, I'll see what Alan wants. If he's legit, I'll bring him here. I'm not risking you." He almost winced when the natural extension occurred to him. "Or the kid."

"You think Alan's part of it." The way she said it was almost accusatory, which was only natural. The safe, normal, civilian world she was equipped to handle just had a helluva jolt, and there was nobody to take it out on but him.

Vincent didn't even mind. If she was bellyaching at him, it meant the emergency was over and she was on the other side, all to the good. "I think it's better safe than sorry. If there were people watching the house, who's to say they aren't watching de la Cruz, too?" The objection was only logical on the surface. He wanted her here, safe and sound, while he pulled a tiger's tail and hopefully cleared up the entire thing.

They could stick him in stockade after, and he could dream about her all he wanted in there. Maybe she'd even write to him.

"That's true." But her expression had closed with an almost audible snap. Those beautiful dark eyes were slightly bloodshot, and she was probably missing her yoga mat. Disruption in routine made everyone cranky. "I still think you shouldn't do this alone."

Maybe she thought she was good backup. The idea that maybe, just maybe, she was feeling charitable or wanted to protect *him* warmed Vince all the way through. "I know what I'm doing. You saw as much last night."

"Yeah, I guess so." Now her big eyes turned haunted, and something was going wrong inside his ribs. "I'm not disputing your capability, Vincent."

"Good." He liked the way she said his name. Just the hint of an accent, as if she'd had French in high school and was letting it out to play. She was probably a whiz with languages. His hands ached, but it wasn't the scratching, itching, flexing need to make a fist. Instead, his fingertips longed to skate over her cheek, and that would lead to leaning in, and maybe he could even get a few moments' worth of heaven for his trouble—if that wouldn't make him a complete creep forcing himself on a helpless woman. *Settle down, Desmarais.* "So you just stay here and watch TV with Eddie, sweetness. Order room service or something."

Her eyebrows shot up. "I don't think that's a service Golden Motels offer." But she smiled, and swung the door fully open.

It was an unexpected victory, and one Vince liked. He followed her into the room. Eddie politely scrambled for the remote to turn down his cartoons, something about an underwater paradise with a big yellow lump cavorting onscreen.

Vincent gulped down a breath and decided what the fuck, he might as well ask. "So, uh . . .when this is all over . . ." *I can't believe I'm doing this.* "Maybe we could, you know . . .what I mean is, you want to maybe get some coffee?"

Cara's mouth softened. Looked like her jaw was preparing to drop; she stopped halfway to the bed and frankly stared at him. "When this is over?"

"Yeah. I mean, you're pretty amazing." *I'm a bastard. I'm a complete fucking creep. She should knee me in the nuts and walk away.* Except she couldn't, and he was the lowest shit on the face of the earth, because he knew as much.

Sure, he hadn't tried to steal a kiss in the bathroom, but this was *so* the wrong time to ask for a date.

Cara studied him for a long, heart-stopping moment. "If this ends up with all of us alive, you can take me out to dinner." Her eyes sparkled. "And you're paying."

"You bet I am." Maybe he was old-fashioned, but some women liked that. Right? "I'm a gentleman."

"I hope so." Now she sobered and her hands came up. She hugged herself, seeking comfort, and his own arms tingled at *that* thought, too. "No, that's wrong. You're a good man, Vincent. Not a lot of people would do this for two strangers."

"Yeah, well." It should have made him feel ten feet tall and bullet-proof, but instead, he almost cringed. He wasn't a fucking altruist, for God's sake. He was a busted-up soldier who had second-guessed his own instincts and nearly got her and a six-year-old ventilated—or worse.

Because he shouldn't have let them stay in Marquez's house. It was a dipshit mistake, and he knew it.

"Vince?" Because she was what Footy Lenz called *a doll* and Grey called a *stone-cold mama*, she took two steps toward him, nervous and delicate as a doe in a hunter's sights, and it looked like she was trying to comfort *him*, of all people. "I mean it. You're pretty amazing. Eddie and I owe you a lot."

Oh, shit. He should just stick to what he knew. Vincent cleared his throat, harshly, and he was a coward twice over, because that stopped her. She stood there and looked at him, and instead of the right thing to say, all he could find in his throat was a dry obstruction and the consciousness of fucking up yet again.

"Thanks," he managed to say, and it sounded sarcastic even to him. "I'm gonna get ready."

IT WAS RIDICULOUSLY easy, which meant his hackles were up. Vincent circled the mission-style church twice, all his antennae out and vibrating. It was the perfect place for a snatch, especially if your target was oblivious—or terrified—enough to walk right up to the front door in a pretty sundress, holding a curly-headed little boy's hand.

Other than that, it was as quiet as . . . well, as a church. It was great terrain, plenty of avenues, but there wasn't a hair out of place. He went in through a side door, marveling at the crappy locks—still, who would steal from God's house?

All sorts of people, that's who.

The building felt deserted. It might have been on the federal historical register, but it was *also* full of mice and guano. He moved from cover to cover, and when he saw the footprints in the dust he felt a grim, grinding satisfaction.

There were at least two assholes inside waiting for someone to waltz in through the front, probably in the nave, but he was going to leave them there holding their dicks. He'd gone just far enough in to figure out the kind of trap it was.

Now he just had to get away without leaving any body parts behind.

He edged down the entry hall, pushed one of the front double doors open—someone had to have unlocked it for the prey—and stepped outside, the wind rattling and stinging with dust. From the top of the wide stone steps you could see the mountains even more clearly; the clouds were slinking across the desert, diamond flashes busily stitching their undersides. It would be nice to be somewhere high up, maybe in a good hotel, having a drink and watching the storm with a dark-eyed woman.

She'd probably put her hair up and wear something classy.

Instinct drove him into a crouch a bare moment before a chunk of the left-hand door evaporated, not because he'd heard the bullet. That was impossible.

No, he went down because the hunted animal in him knew it was too quiet, and his conscious self had only just caught up.

Son of a bitch. He rolled aside, and another confusion of bullets spattered against the doors from the opposite direction. Two shooters inside, maybe more—just as he'd guessed, and maybe they'd heard him moving through the building. The sniper covering the front might have been resting his eyes or just getting Vincent bottled.

They wouldn't shoot her or the kid, would they? He didn't know enough, or he'd guessed wrong. If they'd planned on *him* being here, that meant they could scoop her and Eddie up at leisure.

Which meant Vince had fucked up, again.

More bullets pocked behind him as he scuttled, diving behind a stack of antique wooden pews about to be shredded by flying lead, and Sparky's voice filled his brain. *I won't teach you to bring a knife to a gunfight. I'm gonna teach you to win if you do.*

Vince had a gun, but he was still hoping the old bastard had been right.

Endgame

So Much Therapy

THERE WAS NO yell of *Police, open up!* They didn't knock, just battered down the motel room door. Eddie, frozen on the wrinkled coverlet, screamed and cowered. Cara yanked him down, tumbling off the bed on the other side in a wild tangle of arms and legs. This time, there was no Vincent to save them; she was torn from Eddie's small hands, handcuffed, and carried outside to a squad car, her damp hair swinging and her sock feet hovering above the ground.

She went in on her back and tried to kick out the window before the door on the other side opened and Eddie was thrust through, his hands cruelly zip-tied in front. Shouting, cursing, and static from chattering radios filled the air. The only thing worse than the pain was the *embarrassment*—she'd just been cuffed and thrown into a cop car like a common criminal.

I'm so fired, she thought, inconsequentially, before she realized that was the least of her worries.

Eddie almost spilled into the footwell. Cara flopped, fishlike, and finally managed to sit up; Eddie's hands patted ineffectually at her, trying to help. Peering through the open door on Eddie's other side was a familiar face; she just couldn't remember his name.

It was the younger detective, McIntyre's partner. She found his name with a lunging mental effort—Sanderson, the one who had hovered near the door while she was being questioned, his nose in the air and his questions jabbing at her.

"Mami," Eddie sobbed, and she tried to wriggle into another position somehow, to comfort him. "Mami, Mami, Mami!"

The young detective studied her for a few moments, and she thought she saw a smirk before he slammed the door. Eddie scrambled onto the seat and huddled as close as he could get once Cara finally got herself righted. The young detective slid into the passenger seat, a cop in a regular uniform got behind the wheel, and even if Cara wanted to plead with either of them, she couldn't. There was a window of bulletproof glass behind the thick chickenwire meant to keep criminals where they belonged, firmly in the backseat.

And it was closed.

SHE EXPECTED EDDIE to be torn away, and further expected to be taken to some kind of interrogation where she could explain everything to disbelieving detectives or even federal agents. Maybe she'd even expected a jail cell, but instead, they were both taken through the alley door of an indistinct brick building and down a long hallway, her arms torqued cruelly behind her and Eddie lifted bodily with ruthless efficiency whenever he tripped.

The young detective thrust her into a small, bare, windowless room with a concrete floor, then shoved Eddie in after her. She staggered, numb legs refusing to hold her up; Cara hit the concrete wall, her shoulder giving a burst of hot pain. She was black and blue all over, and had missed her morning practice as well, which just seemed like the final, ironic insult.

Isn't that always the way. A deep, hideous calm descended upon her. She knew the feeling, how could she not? It had shown up once before, when Ben said, *It's actually kind of a relief . . .*

Oh, yes. This was very familiar indeed. The worst had happened, and she was utterly alone.

But not really, because Eddie keened, blundering into her. Every muscle protested, bruises and strained muscles screaming, and she jolted back into her aching skin.

Stop it. You've got to be calm. If you aren't, he's going to lose it. Come on, Cara. Buck up.

"Mami," he sobbed, and she didn't want to correct him. Fuck the agency, fuck their rules, and fuck Marquez for putting a kid through this. To hell with *all* of them.

He was her kid, and it was going to hurt when they took him away. But until then, she would fight.

"Shhh." She closed her eyes, swallowing hard. *First things first.* "Shhh, Eddie. It's all right. I'm here."

That managed to calm him, at least a little. He pressed his face against her side, his trapped fingers worming against her T-shirt. At least she'd been able to take a shower that morning, though any remaining benefit of hot water and relaxation was probably lost.

"Mami," Eddie sobbed breathlessly, a hot dimple of breath just under her ribs.

"I'm right here." Her legs were stiff and with her hands behind her, there wasn't a lot she could do. Still, nothing would get better if she started screaming or thrashing. "Shhh, sweetheart. It's all right. I'm right here."

You're lying. This won't ever be all right. He's going to need so much therapy. So would she, for God's sake.

It took a little while, but he finally stopped sobbing. He just trembled, like a small animal caught in a trap. Cara kept talking, soft soothing nonsense. It was the tone that mattered, gentle and firm, and she wondered blankly what Vincent would do.

He'd have a plan.

Finally, she got Eddie calm enough to sit on the floor. The dark, discolored concrete sloped ever so slightly towards a central drain, and she didn't want to think about why that could be.

Well, she didn't *want* to, but she *did*, and the knowledge was a bucket of ice water poured over her head. She *felt* the chill slide down her body, shoving away the pain, scraping off extraneous considerations.

She was handcuffed in a concrete cube with a single lightbulb in a metal cage overhead. If they turned off the lights she and Eddie would be in the dark, and the thought was another bucketful of chill. She could almost *feel* it gliding over her skin, down the channel of her spine, trickling down her legs to her bare feet.

All right. She imagined Vincent standing in front of her, his head cocked slightly and that odd listening look on his face. *I can handle this. I have to. There's no one else.*

She couldn't hug her kid with her hands cuffed behind her. But she had a solution, one she was amazed she hadn't thought of before now.

"We're going to do some breathing, Eddie. Just like usual." She pushed away from the wall, wincing. "All right? You're going to breathe with me."

"My hands hurt," he sniffled.

The cold wrapped around her, but there was a live coal in the pit of her stomach. If they'd damaged his little fingers, she was going to tear them apart. Cops shouldn't act like this.

Nobody should. But she didn't have time to think about why cops would arrest her and put her in a room like this.

Months of twice-daily practice were about to pay off. Cara crouched, glad her jeans had a little spandex in the weave, and got her right toes hooked on the cuffs. Now she wished she'd dieted a little harder, and her arms squeezed her bruised ribs unmercifully. There were a few bad moments, but then relief threatened to tip her over, because she knew she had a chance.

"Wow," Eddie breathed.

Thanks, kid. Cara choked on a breathy, screamy little laugh. One foot through. She toppled sideways, bracing herself for impact, and almost screamed when she hit the floor.

It took a little huffing and puffing, and tears trickled from under her squeezed-shut eyelids as her shoulders protested, ligament and bone very unhappy and demanding to speak to her manager. But she got her left foot through too, and from there she unfolded, a deep exhalation of relief pouring out and away.

Now, thank God, her hands were in front of her.

She lay on her side, eyes shut tight, and almost sobbed at the release of tension. Eddie monkeyed closer, and she found out they'd cut the zip ties on his wrists before thrusting him through the door.

It didn't change the burning in her stomach, but it was one less problem to deal with.

Those were real cops, or real enough. But someone else is going to pick us up. Bet you any amount of money.

That was one of Ben's sayings, and she was vaguely, oddly glad he wasn't here. Cara lifted her own cuffed hands, examining them in the uncertain light as Eddie helped her sit up. Maybe she could slide them off? She could afford to lose a little skin, and then she'd have her hands free when they came in the door.

It wouldn't do any good, but now she had the illusion of some control and it was easier to think. The squirming panic behind her breastbone vanished.

She might even have figured out getting free of the handcuffs if the door hadn't begun its grating, clanging opening song. Cara scrambled into a crouch, Eddie tucked behind her and peering over her shoulder; when the heavy steel swung on its unoiled hinges, her jaw threatened to drop.

It was Alan de la Cruz, his boot-toes glittering and his smile wide and voracious as ever. He tipped his hat back with one finger, his eyes glittering under the brim's shade, and his black jeans were pristine.

"Alan?" God, she hated how her voice trembled. "What are you—?"

He just stood there, his thumbs stuck in his belt, and she got the idea he was enjoying himself. "I told 'em not to put a scratch on you."

Understanding exploded like a firework inside her skull. Frankly, it almost blinded her. *I was right. This is what you were talking about on the phone.*

You planned *this.*

Oh, the why didn't matter. Not now. All that mattered was figuring out how to keep Eddie safe. "You son of a bitch," Cara husked. *I'm going to kill you. If I can. If God lets me.*

He examined her for a few moments, taking in her dishevelment, the handcuffs, and Eddie's wide, accusing eyes as the boy clung to her side. Finally, Alan shook his head, clicking his tongue like a disappointed grandma.

"You should've just gone to church, chica."

Bad News

INSIDE THE ABANDONED apartment building, piss-soaked refuse crouched in corners, still and silent. It smelled like death and fried food. A small aperture was wiped clean on the dust-choked window. "I don't *know* him," Klemp said, again. "I know Marquez, he had some trouble in Baja last year. Tax and I took care of it so he called me again when he needed extra hands. This kind of work's always a crapshoot. Why didn't you call me before?"

He wasn't quite *nervous*—Klemp was too professional for nerves—but Vince supposed he was hardly comfortable with the situation. Of course, he'd called the man and sworn at him before demanding backup, and that was not a happy way to spend an afternoon after killing two shooters in an old church and flushing out a cowboy-hatted sniper sonofabitch who also packed a revolver.

And now Klemp wanted to know why Vincent hadn't called *earlier*. It boggled the fucking mind.

"Thought you'd be busy." *And I didn't know if you were buddies with de la Cruz, either.* Vincent lifted the monocular to his left eye and squinted. The right side of his face was puffing up and the sutures in his opposite shoulder—the sniper had been the closest thing to professional in that team—would tear if he had to move in a hurry again, but that was unimportant.

What mattered was that Klemp had dropped everything and come running with gear and medi-kit, not to mention transport and ammo. What mattered more was the unassuming brick building across the street, its front a mask of nailed-up boards over broken windows.

What the building contained mattered most of all.

Vincent wanted to go straight through the chained front door and start killing until he found her, but that was stupid. They were almost certainly outnumbered, though probably not outgunned, and she could easily catch a stray bullet. Or if he and Klemp simply blew the building, they'd damage what they wanted to extract whole and well.

Of *course* they'd tracked Cara's phone. If Vince had been a little less arrogant, it would have occurred to him that law enforcement had taps and traces de la Cruz couldn't get his hands on; if the money Alan had been skimming from Marquez's businesses was good for anything, it was good for buying a dirty cop or two. Chatter on Klemp's police scanner had a possible kidnapping at a Golden Motel, and from there it was simply bird-dogging. The official fiction was that suspects had somehow managed to escape in this neighborhood, and the trio of shiny black cars—one sedan, two SUVs—that had just arrived at one of the abandoned tenements was familiar.

Vincent bet if someone ran the plates, they'd come back to Roderigo Marquez. Local police dispatch was trying to make sense of a couple different garbled reports, drawing away the real cops to the west as strange yellow-green storm light filled the deserted, trash-strewn street.

Alan was going to a lot of trouble. The payoff must be huge, hugely personal, or both.

"Too busy to stop you from getting your ass shot off?" Klemp's sigh was a marvel of long-suffering. He was checking gear, wincing every so often as his leg twinged. "When have I ever been too busy for that, asshole?"

"You're a prince," Vincent murmured.

"You're just pissed 'cause they got the jump on you?" Klemp snorted, but he kept moving, checking and laying out gear, stowing, arranging, and just generally doing what he should. "Is that what this is?"

"No." *They have her, and I'm going to get her back. And the kid, because goddammit, she'd want that.* And besides . . .the kid wasn't bad.

He wasn't bad at all. Even kind of reminded Vince of himself at that age. That is, without the whole foster-care-to-juvie-pipeline bit.

"Then what?" Klemp tested the strap on his mapbag, stood up, and settled his tac vest with quick, habitual motions. "Just so I know what I'm gonna get my own ass shot off for."

"Keep bitching and I'll throw you out the window." *Just hold on, sweetness.* The thought of what might be happening to a handcuffed woman inside an abandoned apartment building was not helping him keep his cool. Neither was the thought of someone terrorizing the kid even further.

"Fuck *you.*" Klemp took the mono and shouldered him aside. "Only three cars. We can hit 'em."

I already thought of that, thanks. "And have them call for backup? Two of them are still running. It's transport. We'll hit them en route."

"Unless they're going somewhere with some tight-ass button-down." Klemp stiffened. "Movement. Get suited up, Dez."

"I *am*." He wanted to be watching, but getting into gear had precedence. At least he knew how to do this. His hands didn't itch, and they didn't shake. They moved without his direction, doing the job they'd been trained for. "Keep watching."

"What does it fucking look like I'm doing, ordering tacos?" Klemp let out a low whistle, the mono sealed to his eye. If he noticed the way this place smelled, he didn't mention it. They'd both run lookout in worse. Hell, they'd both *slept* in far, far worse. "*Mamma mia.* Look at that."

Shut the fuck up unless there's something to report. Vince was almost done. Checking, stowing, taping down, spectacles, testicles, ammo, and watch. The old standbys. His nose itched from the dust; he suppressed a sneeze. "What?"

"I can see why you're doing this now." Klemp let out another long low sound, not quite a whistle this time. "Nice legs."

Oh, for fuck's sake. Now was not the time to bounce his knuckles off his buddy's skull and tell him to keep his eyes to himself. "She moving all right?"

"Looks like. They've got her mouth taped." Klemp's voice dropped. It was almost go-time, and he was getting steady. "There's . . .holy shit, there's a kid too."

At least he's alive. "Marquez's." Vincent bounced slightly on his toes, making sure he wouldn't clank and clatter like the Tin Man.

"No shit." Klemp made a single sharp movement, probably wanting to glance at Vincent, but training won out. He kept the mono glued to the scene below. "Putting the packages in the middle car. So that's why you wanted the grenades."

"I'm done with fucking around." Vince's hands kept moving independently of his brain, with thoughtless speed. "Which way are they going?"

"Sir, I'll know once they move, First Lieutenant sir." Not *Sarge*, which would have been pre-game clowning, but actual rank. In other words, Klemp wanted him to get his head on straight. It was as close to saying *you're nucking futs and scaring me, asshole*, as the other man would get.

What would Dr. Karsten say about Vincent now? It wasn't paranoia if the world was truly out to get you, but good luck explaining that to a medic in a safe, comfy little VA office.

"They might be heading to the suburbs," Klemp continued, his free hand resting on his rifle strap. It was a familiar stance; the only thing missing was a wasteland of sand, deep green crowding of jungle, or the shattered remains of what had once been a city and the popping of distant mortars. "That would be nice. In and out, home for dinner."

"We can dream." The knives vanished; Vince checked his vest again, patted down his pockets, and gave one last bounce on his steel-jacketed toes to make sure he wouldn't jingle too badly.

"Go time," Klemp announced. "Repeat, go time. They're pulling out, turning east."

Vincent rolled his shoulders and headed for the door at a good clip. A primer-spotted, battered sedan with a full tank and an engine as babied as its outside was neglected stood ready. If they hustled, they'd be able to tail the motherfuckers. If they didn't—or if Alan kept working smart instead of indulging in more relaxed civilian-hunting—the SUVs would vanish into thin air and Vincent would have lost.

THEY WERE LUCKY; Klemp managed to pull the sedan out of the alley just as the last SUV's taillights winked at the end of the block, turning south. They were also *un*lucky, because Alan and his crew weren't aiming for the suburbs.

They were heading for the desert, and that was bad, bad news.

Far From Helpless

IF IT BOTHERED Alan to be facing them, sitting with his back to the engine on a custom-built bench seat, it didn't show. He'd even buckled Cara in solicitously, running his fingertips over her shoulder and laughing when she flinched. The windows were heavily tinted, and she probably couldn't kick one out with her sock feet.

But she thought about it as Rodrigo Marquez's private, half-limousine SUV wallowed over railroad tracks and headed south on Vitatesca Avenue. They'd hit the freeway soon, if they were going out into the desert.

And God, Cara suspected they were. Eddie shivered, cuddling as close to her as possible, his knees pulled up and one of his old play sneakers untied.

"This shoulda been easy," Alan finally said. His gaze crawled avidly over her torn pink T-shirt, lingered on her chest. "I woulda let you go if you'd just brought the kid."

With the tape over her mouth, Cara couldn't tell him to fuck off and die. Still, he could probably read it in her eyes.

"Still . . .I like you, chica. You got some balls. More than this guy's daddy, that's for sure."

Eddie turned his face into Cara's elbow, pressing in. She wanted to put an arm around him, draw him close. She lifted her hands, a mute entreaty, and restrained the urge to flutter her eyelashes.

Alan's smile was full of a shark's cold good humor. "You want the cuffs off? Maybe in a little bit." He stretched his legs out, taking up plenty of space, those sharp, wicked-gleaming boot-toes near her battered, filthy socks. "When you calm down."

Calm down? Cara could barely believe her ears. *I'll show you calm, asshole. All the way to the end of the block.* A faint sound escaped her throat, and the only shocking thing was exactly how angry she was.

She'd never been this coldly enraged. It flew in the face of every social instinct, every habit pressed into her from childhood to be a good girl, to get along, to think the best of people, to stop mouthing off. It was uncomfortable.

It was also glorious, and she longed to get the cuffs off and fly at him.

Alan's grin widened. "Bet you're pretty pissed. You'll come around, chica. I promise." There was a faint buzzing; he dug in his pocket and fished out a sleek black smartphone. "One second."

Screenglow underlit his face, turning his eyebrows into peaks. Cara glanced down at Eddie, lifting her cuffed hands. Her fingertips worried at the tape over her lips, but after a few moments of tapping at the screen with his thumbs Alan looked back up and poked her knee sharply with one booted toe.

"Now, now. That's insurance, chica." He settled watchfully against his seat again, tucking the phone away. "Man, I got to tell you. Eight years I've worked for that little shit's daddy. Do I get any goddamn recognition? Nada."

Given how this has turned out, I think he should have just plain fired you. Cara glanced at the windows. Thunder rumbled, distant and muffled; the storm was getting closer. This early in the season it might just be a dry one, lightning riding between dust specks, the kind of weather where you could shock yourself hard enough to hurt on any metal appliance or doorknob.

"Anyway, it was supposed to be simple. Papi pays for the little guy, and then—" Alan spread his hands, eyebrows rising again. "Bingo. Everyone's happy."

Cara found herself hoping Marquez was just as dirty as Vincent seemed to think. If he was, he'd probably shoot Alan and fire her, but at least Eddie would be alive.

And she had the unsettling idea she wouldn't mind seeing Alan get shot. Not one bit.

He leaned forward slightly, gaze fixed on her. "But then you had to go fuck everything up, chica. You coulda let the kid go in the parking lot, and nobody had to know anything other than where to deliver the money."

You bastard. If she lunged at him, the seatbelt would catch her. Could she click it off and get across the distance, maybe rake his face with her fingernails?

Vincent would have a better idea. But he wasn't here. Had they shot him at the church they'd expected her to bring Eddie to? Alan hadn't mentioned it, which gave her some faint hope.

Then again, it looked like Dracula Cowboy was good at keeping secrets. There was no way anyone, much less Vincent, could help them now.

"But I suppose it works out." Alan tilted his head as a radio in the front seat crackled, the sound sparking through the half-open privacy window. "Señor gets his boy back, I get the money, and then you and I go down south to a nice little place I know. After a little while you won't even wanna leave."

If her mouth wasn't taped shut, her jaw might have dropped. *Oh, my God, what kind of lunatic are you? I'd never go anywhere with you.*

"I like a little fight in my girls." He glanced at the windows while the SUV slowed, banking like an airplane onto a freeway ramp. There weren't even any red traffic lights, it was a straight shot. If the car stopped, maybe she could have done something. Anything. "Makes it interesting."

You are such *a sleaze*. Cara looked down at Eddie. He watched Alan the way he might a buzzing rattlesnake.

Smart kid.

The driver said something. Alan turned his head and listened, then sighed. "It won't matter." His profile was handsome in the worsening light. "The cops'll pick him up soon enough. Just another washed-out vet."

Vet? Is he talking about Vincent? Hope surged bright and sharp inside her throat, and the fact that it was useless didn't matter. Everything was hopeless; even if Vincent was still alive, he couldn't possibly find them.

But still . . .hopeless, sure, but she wasn't completely helpless. Far from.

Cara lifted her cuffed hands, pointed at her nose, then crossed her palms over her throat, miming suffocation.

Alan studied her, narrow-eyed, for a few moments. "Nah." He shook his dark head. The black cowboy hat lay on the seat right next to him, at least. He was just so . . . so *gauche*. It was the only word that applied. "I don't think I want to see your pretty mouth yet, chica. Might get me distracted." His grin spread again, and Cara glared at him.

All that earned her was a scornful laugh. "Just relax. We'll be there soon."

LIGHTNING PLAYED over the hills, but no rain fell. A dry, warm wind flirted uneasily as a man with a black bandanna over his nose and mouth pulled Eddie bodily out of the car. Cara scrambled to follow, evading Alan's hands, and spilled out onto sand-grimed concrete. She ran straight into the guy holding Eddie, almost bowling him over, and might have made a grab for the gun at his hip if Alan hadn't cracked her a good one on the head.

Cara folded down, her knees meeting dirty concrete with a jolt. Eddie threw his arms around her, screaming.

"*Don't you hurt my Mami!*"

She struggled to stand upright, to throw herself at the staggering asshole, but something else hit her and soupy half-consciousness swallowed her whole.

Collateral Damage

KLEMP'S SEDAN WAS not only hiding a decent engine but also good suspension and all-wheel drive; plus, he was a champion at blending with traffic even when there was none to be found. He was also very good at picking tactical high ground, and even with the killing impatience beating under Vince's skin, he knew enough to shut up and let the other man work.

They trudged just below a sandy ridgeline, making only enough noise to keep away snakes. Vince had only gained a glimpse of their objective before Klemp twisted the wheel and took them off-road with a bounce; now he followed in standard recon pattern, wishing he had a few more of the squad with him. Boom and Grey would be behind Klemp, Tax would be carrying medical gear right after Vince, and last of all would glide silent, efficient Jackson, with his cold eyes and his "exact application of force."

All of them put out to pasture just the way he was at the moment. At least he didn't have to put up with Boom's filthy mouth, or Tax razzing him about falling for a nice girl.

Klemp dropped and scurried for the top of the ridge, hugging cover. Vince followed, careful not to raise too much dust. Not that it mattered—the light was failing, and the stabs of dry lightning made for uncertain visibility.

They reached a tiny divot in the top of the ridge, just right for cradling a couple of assholes who didn't know when to quit. If it started to rain, things were going to get miserable right soon, as Sparky Lee would say.

"Voilà," Klemp muttered, and peered over the top.

The desert wasn't flat; it only *looked* that way if you didn't know what you were doing. Klemp had somehow managed to find the only good vantage point for a few dozen miles, looking down on a sand-choked, blocky concrete complex crouched leonine among sagebrush and clotted boulders. It was a burned-out gas station, and it took a few moments before Vince could see the road that must have run by. Two-lane highway, probably left to rot when the interstate went in.

A single stuttering point of flame flickered in a broken window, just as suddenly extinguished. No discipline; Sparky would have kicked someone's ass for showing that much on a mission. Three gleaming black SUVs were tucked behind the station; a desultory junkyard, also half-marooned in sand, spread behind it. Good cover if they could approach that way.

Cara. Was she still alive? Alan had to have a use for her.

He tried not to think of what that use was likely to be. Maybe they had her to keep the boy contained.

"I hate to ask," Klemp said, softly. "But do you have any fucking idea what's going on?"

"I'm working on it." Vincent shut his eyes, pushed the panic away. It went quietly into the little box, its home while he was on mission.

The familiar killing cold, an old friend, settled over him. It was purely internal, no matter the outside temperature he would still feel this chill. This time, it was dry ice, because Cara was down there and depending on him.

The answer came like a gift, like her shy hands cupping a mug of coffee. Strangely, it arrived sideways, riding a good memory like most flashes of insight. *You're a good man, Vincent . . .not many people would do this for two strangers.*

"Alan wants money. He figures this is a good way to get it." It was ridiculously simple once Vince stopped thrashing, once he was clear and mission-cold again. No doubt old Doc Karsten would be interested in what it took to get a paranoid, junked-out company-grade back on his feet again.

Vincent didn't intend to tell the good doctor that the secret was a woman's dark eyes, her stubborn politeness, and the way she put her foot in his hands, trusting him to lift her safely. "It's also personal," he continued. "It's gotta be. He been working for Marquez long?"

Klemp's relief at Vince suddenly acting like himself was palpable. He wormed the monocular out of its case and studied the ground below. "Eight years? Gotta be." There was no sunlight to flash off the lens, but he was still careful, taking the scene in small sips instead of staring. "Since a couple years before his wife died. Kid was two, three, I think, when *that* happened."

"And Marquez started diversifying after she did, right?" Oh yeah, *now* Vince had the picture.

"I don't know." Klemp turned his head slightly, studying the road leading to the gas station. "But if you say so, I wouldn't bet against it."

Simple. Can't believe I didn't see it before. "Alan was helping him dabble, especially with the arms smuggling. But not getting enough in return, I bet. So he engineered something to keep Marquez held temporarily at or just over the border, thinking he could snap up the kid and get a good chunk of change." *Work it right, and the boss might even think his number two's a hero, getting little Eddie back.*

And Cara? Collateral damage, or just a sweetener to the whole damn deal. Vince was supposed to be collateral damage as well, except Paul would have eventually come looking for him.

By then it would be too late, but Vincent's ghost might have felt some satisfaction.

"I'd'a thought Marquez smarter than that. But he's a civilian." Klemp was now all business. "What do you say we go down, crack the place, and get your girl out?"

My girl. Of course Paul would assume that was the thing getting Vince involved. And of course, he'd be right. A faint sound reached him. Wheels on sand-choked pavement? His eyes snapped open and he edged on his elbows for the top, peering over and letting out a soft, dissatisfied sound. *That's trouble coming.*

Klemp followed his gaze. "Shit."

Headlights, arrowing straight down the road. The solution to the mystery, again, was ridiculously simple once he applied a couple brain cells to it.

Daddy Dearest was coming to pick up his boy.

Too bad Marquez was driving right into a trap. Stealthy movement flickered all through the abandoned station, and Alan had plenty of time for setup.

Vince touched Klemp's shoulder. A few moments later, the hollow at the top of the ridge was empty.

THE SHOOTING started when they were still too far away, and Vincent listened through the sedan's half-open window as he clung to the dash. Thunder rolled over the top of chattering gunfire, and one or two *thumps* were from armaments civilians shouldn't have access to.

In other words, it sounded like a complete and total shitshow, and Vince's only hope was that Cara and Eddie weren't caught in the middle of it. There hadn't been enough time for an exchange; hope was a bright vicious ball of barbwire in his chest.

Of all the things Klemperer liked, driving across rough terrain with no headlights—or headlights taped to slits—was his favorite. Sparky called Klemp a born pathfinder, and it was damn uncanny the way the man could find a route or road where none actually existed. In this case, he took them on a jolting joyride around the ridges, counting on everyone below being too busy to notice.

"Strap in!" Klemp yelled, and cut the wheel. They skidded down the incline, and Vince swore, a steady song as familiar as his breath. The only person who *didn't* cuss when Klemp was driving was Jackson.

Sometimes *that* asshole even slept in the back seat.

They zipped between two towering piles of half-junked cars, lightning flashing in semaphore, and Klemp stood on the brake, the sedan sliding sideways. The car jolted to a stop just as a pillar of light stabbed earthward, and for a moment Vince thought the station had been struck by lightning.

Instead, it was a sleek black helicopter with a floodlight pointed down.

What the fuck? Marquez didn't have that kind of pull, for God's sake.

Klemp cursed, the car rocked to a stop, and Vincent bailed out. It was go time. Now all he had to do was find her; Klemp would watch his back.

And God help anyone who got in his way, because Vincent Desmarais, once again, was ready to kill.

Your Bad Luck

AT LEAST THE ancient walk-in freezer wasn't still active, and the door wasn't hermetically sealed. Cara shoved at it, ignoring the slipperiness of blood on her hands. The cuffs weren't coming off, but the noise outside made that very small potatoes, as Grandma Gemma would say. The only light was from tiny slivers around the door where the rubber seals had cracked and pulled free; there was a Coleman lantern right outside in the hall. Faint random flashes, like people moving in front of the lamp, were probably lightning instead.

Or maybe not, because gunfire interspersed with thunder echoed through the empty gas station. Squat and concrete walled, nothing short of an earthquake would take the building down, which was comforting. The freezer was probably the safest place for them right now, but Cara wanted to know she could get the door open.

Unfortunately, she was having no luck at all. She dropped her shoulder, pushed against it again, bruised feet in socks sliding against smooth concrete and a thin rasping layer of grit.

"What's that sound?" Eddie whispered.

"Thunder," she said, shortly, and pushed once more. Her toes slipped and she slid down, banging her knee and letting out a wounded little cry.

"Mami." He was suddenly there, his little arms around her, trying to hold her up. "That's *guns*. They're gonna kill us."

"Or someone's here to rescue us." *Though your dad might shoot me himself, seeing all this mess.* Her head ached abominably; more blood slipped down her nape, hot and sticky. "Either way, I want to get this open."

"It's locked." But Eddie put his hands flat and pushed while she hung grimly onto the latch, erasing more skin on her toes while she slid. The holes in her socks might even stop the sliding, if she could just—

More gunfire, sharp pops and crackles. There were bigger thumps, and a deep thrumming. She didn't like the sound of *that*. It sounded like a full-scale battle out there.

I hope it's the good guys. Not that she had any idea if there were any good guys in this situation, except one. Then came more hideously loud reports, startlingly close. "Uh-oh." She grabbed Eddie's shoulder with her clumsy, swelling fingers, pulling him back. "Come on."

There were empty, heavy plastic milk crates scattered around, and denuded metal shelves bolted to the concrete floor. She pushed Eddie through the maze, settling him in the very far back corner.

"You're going to hide," she said, with far more certainty than she felt. "We're going to stack these up and you're going to be very quiet and very still." *Like a little mouse in a hole*—should she make it into a game, a reference to one of his library books? At least she wouldn't worry about overdue fines if they survived this, she could probably view every comparatively petty life annoyance with deep serenity. "Don't come out until I tell you it's safe."

Relief filled Eddie's round little face. If she knew what to do, he was all right. Her conscience pinched—none of this was safe, she had no damn clue, and she was basically lying to a six-year-old who trusted her.

Did Grandma Gemma ever feel like this, raising little Cara? Nothing was safe, the world was a giant grinding maw, and they were shreds of flesh and bone caught in the teeth.

Especially if Alan won the fight. She couldn't see what was going on, and the uncertainty sickened her. Her hands threatened to shake, and the blood dripping down her neck was concerning.

She couldn't remember eating or sleeping, now. It felt like she'd been terrified, jumping from one evaporating stepping-stone to another, for a very long time.

Cara stacked all the plastic crates and other refuse she could find, as well as a couple manky old cardboard boxes, around Eddie; she pressed a kiss onto his sweating forehead. "I love you," she said, fierce and low, as there was another crescendo of fire outside. It sounded like it was getting closer. "I love you *so much*. Everything is going to be all right."

"I love you too." And bless him, it sounded like he meant it. "You're my Mami."

We'll cover that later. Cara kissed him again, then stacked the remaining camouflage. It wouldn't take long for anyone to find him, but maybe they'd get a miracle. "Be very still, and very quiet now."

He nodded, then he was lost in the gloom. Cara picked up the last empty milk crate and retraced her steps to the door.

I'm about to kill someone with a plastic bin college kids used to put records in. Her lips moved soundlessly. She gripped the crate, her fingers numb. *They're going to shoot me and take Eddie anyway.*

It didn't matter. The world had gone mad, but her tiny corner of it was very simple right at the moment.

More shots, closer together. Shadows moved between the lantern and the door. There was a rattle—he'd chained the door shut, the fucker.

Cara raised the crate. A thin trickle of blood slid down her right forearm, a hot questing fingernail. She calculated where the door would swing, and when it did, she blinked furiously, dark-adapted eyes suddenly welling with hot salt water as the light scorched them.

A sob caught in her throat. It was Alan, his hat gone and his hip-length leather jacket torn. One of his toe-caps had been ripped off, his hair stood up wildly in all directions . . .

. . .and the gun in his hand was pointed straight at her. The hole at the end of the barrel looked huge, and very black.

"Oh, chica," he said softly, musingly. "You got some bad luck."

A GUNSHOT BOUNCED off concrete; a bright muzzleflash painted the walls.

Friendly

IT WASN'T A FIREFIGHT, it was a pitched fucking battle, and the only thing saving their dynamic-duo asses was that both sides were too occupied with each other to notice a pair of jokers in the deck.

Klemp ducked into cover, Vince followed a half-breath later, fetching up against concrete with a rattling thump. The station's back door was ajar, vibrating a little as soundwaves brushed it with violated air. He thumped Klemp's shoulder, both their mouths gapped a little so the explosions didn't flex eardrums too badly, and they took the door the way they'd taken too many others to count.

Inside was a short hallway, a manager's office on one side, storerooms on the others. The footing was good, though the place was cluttered with trash; the abandoned station was too isolated for teenagers to gather around bonfires and shag in the back rooms.

The 'copter was worrisome. If Marquez had that kind of pull, he wouldn't have been arrested in the first place; if it was Alan's, he wouldn't have sent the dumbasses in the parking lot or a single six-man team to the house. There were too many players on the board, meaning more stray lead flying around.

And *that* meant a higher chance of civilian casualties.

He and Klemp leapfrogged down the hall, covering each other without words and with barely a shared glance. Like clockwork.

Then they turned the corner, and Klemp's rifle spoke once, twice. The dark shape with a familiar, battered cowboy hat in front of the freezer door spilled to the ground, a puppet with all its strings cut, and Vince had his rifle pointed at the asshole's backup.

Or, maybe not backup, because they were in full SWAT gear coming down the hall in standard *let's not fuck this up* formation, and second in line was a semi-familiar face greased with sweat and creased with uncomfortable-looking helmet straps.

Graying, heavyset Detective McIntyre stared at Vincent, his sidearm held low and ready. If he was surprised, it didn't show. Rather, he looked like he'd just had a helluva good idea and was turning it over inside his head to check for holes.

What the fuck is going on?

It didn't really matter, he decided. Vincent's finger tightened on the trigger. The SWAT guy in the lead was shouting, and if that greased-up tac-suited wannabe so much as *twitched* he was going to get ventilated along with the rest of his buddies. It hit him then, the way things did during a mission when your brain suddenly found a sliver of processing power because time had become all bendy—Klemp had just shot Alan de la Cruz.

And there was only one reason for de la Cruz to be back *here,* near what had to be a walk-in freezer.

God, what do you say? She's one of yours, why don't you throw me a little break here?

Thunder rumbled. There was a final spattering of gunfire, and radio chatter bounced through the hallway's confines.

Behind Vince, a woman screamed. Detective McIntyre deliberately, slowly, holstered his piece; he shouted into his crackling radio. Then, the cop shouldered the SWAT leader aside, and Vincent realized he was lowering his own rifle.

A washed-up, trigger-happy, paranoid vet would have wasted them all and moved out to take care of the rest of the world. But a sober professional could tell the threat was diminishing, even if the woman behind him kept screaming, a broken sob at the end. Something clattered, but Klemp was in there and the sound wasn't combat.

So McIntyre was the clean cop, or at least clean*er*. Or if he wasn't, he had something planned for Vincent that wasn't shooting him, and Vince needed to figure out what that was.

Vincent also realized Cara wouldn't have a clue who the hell Klemp was. At least he could be sure Paul wouldn't hurt her or Eddie, and if there was any Alan-related backup there—probably not, it didn't seem as if de la Cruz would like sharing—it was dead now.

It sounded like Cara was very much still moving and conscious. Relief rose hot and sour in his throat, and Vincent's jaw was an iron bar, his teeth aching.

"*Friendly,*" McIntyre yelled, his arms up and his big body inserted gingerly between Vince and the SWAT team. The man had some balls, that was for sure. "Fucking *friendly*, you asshole, put that down! Put it down! *Down*!"

I am, you idiot. But if you try to arrest me, I swear to God you'll lose your entire fucking team.

What came out of Vince's mouth, in a breathless-soft valley between rolls of thunder and the shearing thop-thop of the 'copter as it wheeled out into the desert, was something else. "Took your damn time, Detective."

"Fuck off." McIntyre clapped the SWAT leader—a big husky blond fellow—on the shoulder, gingerly. "Ease down, Jim, he's not one of theirs. Everyone just *calm the fuck down.*"

There was another short clatter from the freezer. "God *damn* it," Klemp shouted, his voice echoing. "I'm here to *help* you, for God's sake!"

It didn't sound like she was going to listen. Girl had some guts, indeed.

"How many?" McIntyre barked.

"One buddy. Two civilians. Three total." Adrenaline smoked coppery on Vincent's palate; he hoped like hell the kid was alive and in there with Cara. "Get some medical out here, they probably weren't gentle. Marquez?" Thunder almost swallowed the last word.

McIntyre shook his head, his mouth turning down, and for a moment he looked even older and more cynical, if that were possible.

Well. That answered *that* question. And apparently good old Mac here had pieced together a few things on his own, and wasn't suspecting Vincent. Or, if he was, he had a cool enough head to talk everyone down and *then* sort things out.

Which made him better than a few COs Vince had suffered service under.

"*Vince*!" Klemp yelled, and there was a clatter. "Get in here!"

As soon as I can. He had to make sure this man and his buddies weren't a threat to *her*. "You gonna arrest us, McIntyre?"

"Not unless you make me." The old detective's expression was almost too sour to be believed. "Jim, for fucksake, get us medical out here, willya?"

"Ten-four." The SWAT leader finished lowering his rifle, and his team relaxed a fraction. They looked like good puppies, well-trained, and the two in the key positions were slighter and shorter.

That was good. Women had better reaction times, and they were a little less likely to go trigger-happy.

Just a little, though. And when they did go, watch out.

There was another scraping crash from the freezer. "*Owwwww*," Klemp howled.

Vincent turned, his back roughened with gooseflesh at the thought of their weaponry behind him. He toed the freezer door a little wider, stepped over Alan's twitching body, and restrained the urge to kick the fucker as he did so. *Looking for an easy payday, huh? And you had plans. I hope you're in hell, and that you tell them one of my men sent you.*

"Cara?" he said into the darkness. "Cara, sweetness, it's Vince. It's friends, we're friendly. Calm down."

Something large whizzed past his head; he ducked reflexively but didn't bring his own rifle up.

It was only a milk crate.

"I'M SORRY," SHE repeated. Eyes wide, her entire body trembling, she wiped at her mouth with the back of one blood-grimed hand. Her socks were in tatters, her T-shirt was in rags, her hair was a wild glory, and she kept shaking away from the EMTs to look for Eddie. "I thought you were . . .I'm so sorry."

Klemp wasn't going to hold a grudge, but he wasn't exactly mollified. "First time I've ever been hit in the head with a goddamn milk crate," he muttered, then caught himself as Vincent glared. "It's okay, ma'am. Things were a little hectic in there."

The 'copter was police-issue. A few of Alan's little helpers had survived and were under arrest, a good half-dozen of Marquez's hired backup were as well. It hadn't been a two-party tango but three, or three and a sliver if you counted Klemp and Vince.

In short, the paddywagons were all but bursting at the seams, and a short, no-nonsense EMT with a blonde ponytail and wide green eyes shone a penlight in Klemp's eyes, checking pupil reactions. He'd caught the corner of a crate on one side of his head, and head wounds were messy.

Cara looked like she'd been through a grinder, and her feet were so battered it was amazing she'd been upright at all. The handcuffs had cut her wrists cruelly, blood painted her face and clotted in her hair, and she probably had a concussion to top it all off.

Vincent's hands tingled. The rage was back, circling him, and the only thing that kept it throttled was the fact that Alan was in a bodybag and she was, after all, alive.

"You coulda called me." Detective McIntyre had lost the helmet and was working on the body armor; the tac gear was probably pinching in a few indiscreet spots. Lightning painted his sweating face with garish glow for a moment, and it smelled like they were just a few minutes ahead of the rain. "Gave you my card and everything."

"Couldn't tell which one of you was bought." Vince knew he should have been conciliatory. He should have been pumping the guy's hand and singing *gee thanks*, but somehow, he didn't feel like it. "You *or* your nice young partner."

"Six years I've worked with him, since he was a baby deet." McIntyre dug in his pocket, fished out a battered pack of Lucky Strikes. "He slept on my couch during his divorce, the asshole. Prison's too good for the fucker."

Apparently Sanderson had been paid off first by Marquez under Alan's direction, then by Alan himself, and was only too happy to oblige his banker. Maybe the man even had reasons, but all Vince knew what that if by some fluke he met Sanderson on the street, it wasn't going to end well.

For the cop, that was.

"Eduardo's going to be all right," another EMT said to Cara, gently. This one was a skinny redheaded guy; his name tag said *Gemmell.* "See? He's a tough kid, just a couple bumps and bruises, like from playing outside. Now we have to look at you, ma'am."

Eddie wriggled as close to Cara's side as possible. She settled, her shoulders dropping, and glanced guiltily at Vincent.

He nodded. *It's safe, sweetness.*

The relief printed on her battered face was instant, warm, and felt so good a lump rose in his throat.

"This one's okay." The blonde EMT nodded sharply, clicking the penlight off and waving Klemp aside. There were relatively few injuries on the cops' side; they were just cleanup, after all. "Sir? We need to get these two on the road for the hospital. Especially her."

Eddie wasn't asking about his dad. Vincent didn't want to be the one to tell him *he was coming for his boy, and he got shot.*

Not yet. And certainly not in those terms.

"I'm going with her," Vincent said. Softly, but the command was unmistakable. "Klemp'll follow in his car."

"Still don't trust me, huh?" McIntyre's smile was a marvel of bitterness. He dug in one pocket, fishing out a pack of cancer sticks, then in another, looking for a lighter. "Christ, doesn't anyone smoke anymore?"

"It's a good thing I didn't trust you." Vince folded his arms. His own bruises ached, and when the chemical cocktail of combat wore off pretty soon, he was going to feel like shit.

But he was alive. So was Eddie. And most importantly, so was Cara.

McIntyre shook his head and turned away, barking orders and still searching through his pockets for a light. Jim, the blond SWAT leader, eyed Vince for a moment and followed, reluctantly. A quiet guy, and the way he moved shouted he'd been in the service, too.

Which was probably why he hadn't popped a few into Vince. Trigger discipline in that guy's unit must be tighter than normal.

"I'm really sorry," Cara said again. "Mr. Camp? I'm really sorry. I just . . . I thought—"

"Don't worry about it." Amazingly, Klemp was grinning, white bandage tape glaring on his forehead. A few heavy raindrops scattered, pocking onto concrete and sending up tiny puffs of dust. The desert was about to get a drink after a hard summer's work. More lightning flashed. "Get on up in the ambulance, ma'am. Can't wait to be introduced properly. Vince's gonna marry you, you know."

For fuck's sake. Thunder arrived; the storm was closing in. "Klemperer, get the goddamn car." Vince's tone gentled when Cara's gaze jolted in his direction. Those big, dark eyes pulled on every string in him and the fear came back with its sharp teeth, as diamond-hard as the lightning beginning to flicker in earnest, drawing ever closer.

"Lie back," the redhead said to her. "Let's get you to the hospital, ma'am. And the little guy too."

Cara closed her eyes, swaying on the gurney, and Vincent lunged for her. But it was the EMT who caught her, guiding her down, and a few more of them clustered, sensing distress. Vince scooped up Eddie instead, and followed when the medics began to hustle. The little boy buried his face in Vince's neck, and they were both, for once, probably hoping for the same thing.

We'll See

THE STING OF A needle in her arm, the sense of being lifted, a grateful velvet darkness closed around her. Cara floated for a long while; bits and pieces of talk floated with her.

"—real name's Albert Jones, lately from a nice little suburb in Minneapolis. Young man went west and turned it into *de la Cruz* before he hooked up with Marquez." An asthmatic smoker's wheeze lingered at the end of the sentence, and Cara's eyelids rose. Hazy indistinct light flooded her brain.

"Albert? No wonder he changed it." That was Vincent, soft and amused, and a fuzzy relief poured through her. He was alive, and if he was here, it meant she was safe.

But where was Eddie? Would CPS take him? She had to explain, she had to fix it. He'd be so scared.

"Yeah, well." The detective coughed. It was McIntyre, and that also meant she was safe, right? If Vincent was talking to a detective, it meant . . .what? "We think he's the one that hired out the hit on Amelia Marquez, or at least facilitated it. He got Roderigo into the illegal bullshit afterward; it's Amelia's money they used to prime the pump."

"Figures." Cloth shifted. Sounded like Vincent was pacing. She could imagine him moving restlessly, light on his feet for such a big man. "When did Marquez find out Alan was skimming?"

"We don't know yet. Looks like he was planning to take de la Cruz out quietly in Mexico, but the fucker beat him to the jump on this side and was using cops to do it." The older man coughed, deep and racking, and there was a cellophane crackle.

Amusement colored Vincent's voice, deep and rich and restful. "Smoking's gonna kill you, you know."

McIntyre didn't like the news. "If I wanted a mother, I'd go visit mine."

The blackness came back, and Cara fell into it without a murmur.

WHEN HER EYELIDS drifted up again, the world was much clearer.

She stared until she realized she was looking at a hospital ceiling, dimmed lights buzzing faintly. Amazingly, she felt no pain, just a warm fuzzy blanket of chemical sedation.

It took work to turn her head. It was a nice room, and she wondered how she was going to pay for this privacy on her salary before she realized she was probably out of a job. A utilitarian hand-washing sink dimpled a long pink counter to her right; the door to the bright hallway lingered slightly open. A slice of warm electric light came through, making a strange shape on the wall and a door that was probably a small closet for medical supplies; the gleam of a small bathroom was visible behind the opening's shadowing shelter.

The window was full of nighttime and occasional bright flashes. Rain rustled and spattered, a regular gullywasher. Out in the desert, flash floods would eat at the sides of canyons, and for a brief moment before winter everything would green. A television flickered mutely on an armature across the room, a blonde news anchor's neutral-lipsticked mouth moving solemnly as footage of moving water played, a car sliding away under its chocolate surface as the owner, dragged to safety, clung to a pair of husky firemen.

So someone else had been rescued, too.

A pink-flowered, vinyl-covered settee was pulled up next to the bed, a courtesy for visitors. It was too small for the man sprawled on it, his limbs contorted uncomfortably. Not only was he too tall and wide for the perch, but he was also cradling a curly-headed six-year-old. Eddie's thumb was in his mouth, and he had light bandages around his wrists. He was sleeping soundly, deeply, and so was Vincent.

Both of them were probably exhausted. It was the first time she'd seen Vincent asleep; without his usual pained watchfulness, his mouth had relaxed. It did good things for him. A faint bump in his proud nose showed where it had been broken once, and his bruised, scraped hand gently cupped the back of Eddie's head. If the kid tried to roll away Vincent would curl around him protectively; you could see as much.

They looked, all things considered, very comfortable.

A deep sigh worked out of her. One moment Vincent was asleep; the next, his eyes snapped open. Nothing else on him moved, and his breathing stayed exactly the same.

How did you learn to do something like that? She was exhausted just *thinking* about it.

They gazed at each other for a long, taffy-stretching, silent moment. The window flashed with lightning, a cup trembling-full, but the thunder was faraway and could barely get through the bulk of the hospital.

"Hi," she managed, in a sleepy, slurred little voice. Her tongue was dry, and didn't want to work quite right.

"Hi, yourself." The corners of his mouth tilted up a little, and his voice was a comforting rumble. "Everything's all right."

Are you sure? Cara managed to lift her right hand, stared at her fingertips. Bandaging wrapped tightly around her wrists. There was a needle in the back of her hand, and the IV pole next to the bed held a bag of clear liquid. "Eddie?" she whispered.

"He's fine. Worn out." Vincent paused, tucking his chin slightly as if he could get a glance at the kid but stopping when he realized it was impossible. "Nobody's gonna take him away, sweetness. You can rest easy."

I wish I could believe you. But at least for the moment, he was safe. She sagged against the pillows. "Marquez?"

A faint groan of thunder swallowed the tentative silence. Vincent shook his head slightly, his stubble rasping against Eddie's curls.

Cara let out a soft, dreaming sound. Was it wrong to feel so relieved? Probably.

"You were pretty banged up." Vincent's tone was soft, even. His thumb moved slightly, a soothing little motion against Eddie's head. "I shouldn't have left you."

There was no way either of them could have known. But she had other questions. "How . . .how did Alan . . ." *How did they find us?*

"Cops traced your phone. One of the detectives—Sanderson—was his dirty little helper." A faint edge of anger sharpened the words, immediately contained when Eddie stirred. When he settled again, Vincent continued, but much more softly. "Don't worry about it. It's all tied off, just rest."

"Eddie . . ." Her eyes blurred. *It's impossible. They won't let me take him. They probably shouldn't, I'm a terrible mother.*

"McIntyre—the detective—talked to a judge. CPS has done an interview or two. You're already a pretty good bet since the agency did a background check. Temporary, but you can relax. He's not going anywhere." Vincent paused. "Neither am I."

The world wavered, but not because of the medication. Instead, it was the lens of tears, distorting everything. One slow fat drop trickled down her temple, into a bandage. She could feel it stuck to her hair, glued with dried disinfectant. The entire world smelled like pain, copper, and nose-stinging antibacterial stuff. "Oh."

"Jesus, don't cry." Vincent tensed, but his words were slow, quiet, even. "I know we don't know each other very well, and if it doesn't work out, okay, that's fine, we'll at least be friends. But I'm not gonna let anything happen to you. Or to him, either."

How strange. Cara's mouth trembled. *I want to believe that too.*

"Anyway." Did he sound, of all things, *nervous*? "I figure if you can take on armed men with a milk crate, the least I can do is buy you dinner."

Oh, yeah. That. "Your friend," she whispered. She'd done her best to lay the guy flat. "Is he . . ." *Is he hurt?*

"Klemp? Oh, yeah. He likes you." A smile crept over Vince's mouth. She watched, fascinated, because it held no bitterness at all. "Says he wants to be best man at the wedding."

"Wedding?" *Oh, my God.* Maybe it was the pain meds. Maybe she was dreaming.

Maybe she was dead, and they were trying to figure out just where to put her.

Vincent almost shrugged, caught the motion just in time. Eddie stirred once more, and they both held their breath until he went boneless again, relaxing against a broad chest. Warm and safe, and utterly unconcerned.

It looked nice. If Cara could never feel that way again, at least *he* could.

"Well," Vincent said finally. "Klemp's an optimist. But I've got to tell you, that's what I'm intending. If, you know, you can stand me."

It's fifty-fifty, dead or dreaming. A thread of thin, unhealthy laughter boiled up from Cara's midsection, caught in her throat, and turned into a sour, soundless burp. "We'll see," she said when it died, swallowing hard. Her eyelids were made of lead now, and drifting down. She could fight, but what was the point?

Finally, at last, she was safe. As safe as possible.

"Yes, we will," Vincent echoed, quietly. And then she was gone.

Home at Last

Six months later

THE *FOR SALE* SIGN was finally gone, just a square divot in the front yard to show where it had stood sentinel. The choice had come down to another faux-adobe—much smaller than Marquez's luxurious compound, to be sure—and this trim yellow two-story with its white shutters and landscaped dry-garden full of native succulents. The backyard had a tiny strip of grass that required watering, but every kid needed some lawn.

Come next summer, Eddie would love playing catch out there.

Cara hit the garage door opener and pulled into now-familiar dimness. It looked like the boys had put a dent in unpacking the stacked boxes; Vincent's weight set and treadmill were almost excavated. It was amazing—and faintly disturbing—how much of her old furniture, her old *life*, was in storage, just waiting to be repurposed.

She cut the blue Volvo's engine and sighed, massaging her temples; the scar at the back of her head was still a little tender sometimes. This was a nice boxy car, but sometimes she missed the Rover's height. It was good to have an automatic, though. She hated manuals.

The kitchen door opened and a familiar pair of dark eyes peered out. Eddie stood on tiptoe to reach for the button; it was his job to "secure the door." He took to it seriously, too, biting his lip and punching with gusto.

The temporary order was well on its way to being permanent; overworked and underpaid bureaucracy considered a vet with a good service record and a "childcare professional" to be a good and above all easy solution, especially with a detective—McIntyre showed up at every hearing, bless him—vouching for them.

Eddie's new therapist Miranda said the lack of nightmares was a good thing. She also said Cara didn't need to worry so much; time and steadiness would work its own wonders. *The important thing is that he knows he's loved*, she said, peering over the top of her steel-rimmed glasses, and Cara's throat had filled with a nameless weight.

Who *couldn't* love him? Especially when he hopped down the stairs, throwing his arms around her middle and crowing with delight. "Mami's home! Mami's home!"

It was his regular greeting.

"Oof." Cara swayed, hugging him just as fiercely. "You're getting so tall."

He did his level best to squeeze the breath out of her. "Didja get milk? I'll carry the milk."

"I could never forget the milk." *Especially with you putting it on the list, ten feet high.* He was taking well to public school, too; he had a glaring crush on his teacher, Miss Morden. Cara hitched her purse strap higher on her shoulder and popped the trunk, settling a single gallon of milk in Eddie's waiting arms. She hadn't even had time to take a shower at the studio and was still in her tank top and yoga pants, but the end of February was raw enough she needed a jacket past sundown. "Go slow, all right?"

"Yes ma'am." He nodded gravely and set off. Another shadow filled the garage door.

"Hey, you." Vincent held the door wide for Eddie, watched to make sure he got up the wooden step into the kitchen, and strode along the car's side. "How was class?"

"Good." That was, in fact, why she was twenty minutes late; Sarah had collared her after she finished teaching the hatha intensive. "They're talking about giving me another couple slots; they keep filling up."

"I know I'd take a few, just to watch you." He grinned and subtracted the paper grocery bag from her, deft as usual. "I'll carry this. Go in and wash up. Dinner's almost ready."

I'm getting spoiled. She slammed the trunk, and it was good that the noise didn't make her flinch. Progress was being made. "Are we seeing Klemp?" Paul had forgiven her entirely for the milk-crate thing, though he joked about her temper. There was a family reunion back in Oregon; he had an early flight.

"He's setting the table. Bitching the entire time." Vincent's hair was growing out, and he had largely lost the haunted look. His last checkup had gone well, too. *I'm not going back on duty,* he'd said quietly into her hair last night, his hand spread against her hip, warm and sure in the darkness. *The doctor's on my side, might as well let him do his job.* "He flies out tomorrow morning. I'm taking him to the airport, then I'll take Eddie to school."

"I can take him." Cara caught at her purse as it slipped again, wishing he'd let her carry at least some of the groceries.

"No, *you're* sleeping in. It's your turn." Vince didn't seem too worried. There was his pension, and sometimes he mentioned *the private sector, if we need the money.*

Cara wasn't so sure what she thought about that. But Eddie was in the door again, bouncing from foot to foot. It wasn't just her imagination, he was a little taller. "It's barbecue time," he piped, eager and excited. "Papi even let me hold the tongs."

"Are you sure that's safe?" She followed Vincent. He wouldn't even let her lift a box, if he could help it.

And Eddie was calling him *Dad.*

"Man's gotta learn sometime." Vincent turned sideways, hefting both bags, to get through the door. "Get the silverware, Eddie. You go wash up, sweetness."

"Yes, sir." A laugh surprised her, jolting free, she paused on the wooden step, one hand on the doorjamb, and closed her eyes.

Clink of silverware, excited murmurs, a lovely smell of dinner wafting through the house. It was as far away as possible from a sterile, breathlessly tense mansion, and if Eddie missed his race car bed and his father, he made no sign of it.

Kids are resilient, his therapist said. *He's doing fine.*

He still crawled into bed with Cara most nights, wedging himself between her and Vincent as tightly as possible. He clung to her when it was time to go to school, and rarely let go of Vincent's hand in public. When he mentioned Marquez at all, it was *my other dad.* And during thunderstorms, he covered his eyes and trembled like a tiny animal in a trap.

"Hey."

She opened her eyes.

Vincent stood, haloed by warm golden kitchen light, his hand out. "You all right?"

"Just fine," she said, blinking furiously. "Thinking."

"You think too long, it'll get cold. Come on."

She laid her hand against his. Warm and safe, and sure. If *he* had nightmares, he kept them to himself, and his touch was always gentle.

Cara took a deep breath, closed her fingers around his, and stepped into the light.

Home at last.

finis

Biography

"LILITH SAINTCROW lives in Vancouver, Washington, with her children, dogs, cat, a library for wayward texts, and assorted other strays."

CPSIA information can be obtained
at www.ICGtesting.com
Printed in the USA
FSHW011338200321
79663FS